Riding the Float

DORIS WILBUR

an imprint of Sunbury Press, Inc.
Mechanicsburg, PA USA

an imprint of Sunbury Press, Inc.
Mechanicsburg, PA USA

For information about special discounts for bulk purchases, please contact Sunbury Press Orders Dept. at (855) 338-8359 or orders@sunburypress.com.

To request one of our authors for speaking engagements or book signings, please contact Sunbury Press Publicity Dept. at publicity@sunburypress.com.

ISBN: 978-1-62006-346-0 (Trade paperback)

Library of Congress Control Number: 2019950153

FIRST MILFORD HOUSE PRESS EDITION: September 2019

Product of the United States of America
0 1 1 2 3 5 8 13 21 34 55

Set in Bookman Old Style
Designed by Crystal Devine
Cover by Terry Kennedy
Edited by Lawrence Knorr

Continue the Enlightenment!

This book is dedicated to my family—
my husband, Jerry, and children:
Susan, Mark, Eric, Krista, and Virgil,
who have lived with and supported
my creative endeavors for many years.

I hope it will inspire awareness of the
modern world around each of us now.
May it be a gentle nudge
to prompt personal action
by the reader to do something,
anything to make it a better place
for this and future generations.

Chapter One

SUGAR CREEK sparkled in the sun as it wound its way through a verdant valley then on to the Susquehanna River. Hilltop Farm was surrounded by pastures, fields, and woods and sat high above the stream catching the morning sun plus witnessing specular sunsets. Ben Carlisle had grown up there on the 120 acres and worked the small dairy every day with his father before he died when Ben was only 23. His mother had died years before of a stroke and as the only son, he had inherited the house, a big rambling barn, a few outbuildings, the chicken house, the machinery shed, and an old outhouse no longer needed. He had an assortment of machinery to work the farm too, a Farmall Tractor with a plow and harrows, a mowing machine, side rake, baler, grain drill, chopper, and a rickety hay wagon. His dairy consisted of 56 Holstein cows, a few middle-aged now, most only a few years old.

Ben lived alone on the farm since Amy his older sister had married Warren Bedford, a dairy farmer across the valley who was not only Ben's brother-in-law but a good friend too. Amy was seven years older than Ben and she and Warren had a son named Kasey.

Ben had not only inherited everything on the farm however, he was also shocked by the debt he inherited from his Dad too. He had been behind in his taxes, feed bill and still had a balance due on some farm equipment before he passed. Ben needed money to take care of those pressing bills but couldn't sell the machinery. He needed the equipment to work the fields and harvest feed for the dairy. So, he was forced to sell off almost half of the cows just to get his father's old debt off his shoulders to keep the farm going. He kept 30 cows, a little more than half his herd, so there'd be a milk check coming in and it should hopefully be enough to support him for a while if he lived frugally. He planned on building the herd back up by getting some of the cows bred so he'd have new heifers in the spring to raise into more milkers. If he got any bull calves, he'd have them castrated to turn them into steers and sell them off for beef after two years. He wanted heifers though. His dream was to have a large dairy, hire help and expand the farm into a very profitable operation. He also wanted to add a few more acres to his property sometime in the future, so he'd be able to plant more crops and have lots of pasture for his cows, then he'd have a great place to raise a family and something wonderful to hand down to his sons or daughters when they got married and had a family of their own.

There was no extra money in his budget to hire help, so Ben struggled for a few years trying to get the crops planted and harvest them all on his own. He also had to do the milking in the morning and again in the evenings without help. At night, he'd fall into bed totally exhausted. The house looked like the bachelor's hang out it was. Often there was no time for proper grocery shopping or doing any sort of housekeeping. If his Mom could see how much he'd let the dust collect in the house and his bachelor style of not cooking a healthy meal, she would have given him an earful. Most nights he was so tired he just made himself a bowl of Ramen Noodles or gulped down a quick-frozen dinner then called it a day. He thought at times about giving it all up, selling the cows and machinery then getting a factory job, but this was the life he loved, being his own boss and working with the animals while spending most of his time outdoors. The thought of being shut inside most of the day working for someone else week after week scared him. He liked his independence and freedom plus being outdoors most of the time. So, he kept working long grueling hours on his own in the hopes of making the farm profitable.

Ben had met Karen at a birthday party for his nephew Kasey. She worked in an office with his sister Amy and she had been invited to the party also. She wasn't a country girl though, and that troubled him a little at first. She had been raised in the suburbs where the lawns were neatly mowed, roads and driveways were paved, and kids played video games most of the time or rode bikes in the streets. She had several stores nearby along with lots of fun things to do. He had thought when he chose a wife it should be one who knew of the demands living on a farm and could do the hard work involved, but Karen stole his heart right from the start, and she was open to living the life Ben talked about.

She was smart enough to have a career job of her own and certainly with her looks she could pick someone else to marry, but she fell for Ben as much as he fell for her. After Ben showed her the farm and she got used to being near the large cows, she took to being out there away from town right away.

"You own all this land Ben?" she asked amazed when he showed her his fields and pastures along with the woods one day. Her home had consisted of a single-story home, with an attached garage and a small yard which could be mowed in less than half an hour if you walked slowly. When she looked out her windows on either side there was another house right beside hers. She told Ben it was a good neighborhood, nonetheless, one neighbor played loud music late into the night quite often. Another had parties where the police had to be called because they drank too much, and a fight always broke out.

She added there was a couple across the street who argued loudly regarding the lack of money every month when the bills were due. Cars ran up and down the streets at all times of the night and day, and streetlights were always glaring right outside her window at night she told him. There was no privacy there such as he had on his farm. The neighbors where Amy lived knew everyone's business, when they were coming and going, having visitors or anything happening in their lives.

"And Ben," she said, "out here you don't have any dogs pooping on your lawn you have to clean up after."

Ben winced and said, "Oh, there's poop here Karen, lots of it," he said thinking of the cows and smiling. She was so damn cute he thought and naïve too, but in a refreshing way.

He was so familiar with the farm girls he had gone to school with the thought of them as almost sisters and not romantic possibilities. He'd spent time growing up with them from elementary school to high school graduation and they were around him when he went through his geeky awkward stages along with acne and the stupidity adolescents have. He wanted a woman who thought of him as the man he now was. He had dated a few other women, some very attractive and nice, however, none seemed right to him and a couple was what he thought of as "high maintenance types" he was sure they'd never stick it out on the farm. They weren't the type he needed as a partner, so he stayed a bachelor for quite a while until he met Karen.

He was so in love with her she could have been totally unskilled at everything a woman needed to be a good partner, but she wasn't. Karen was fit and athletic before they married she ran, not walked, the family dog around the blocks where she lived every day. She had long brown hair that fell halfway down her back, which she often wore in a single braid. He loved her dark brown eyes too, and the way she looked at him so lovingly. She was beautiful to him even though she wore very little makeup. Karen laughed easily at his silly jokes or dumb mistakes. She was good at taking care of her younger brothers and sisters and compassionate to the elderly people at the Senior Center where she volunteered.

Karen was a friend and blessing for him and besides knowing how to cook, which he sure didn't have the patience for, she had studied accounting and could budget the home and farm expenses. She actually enjoyed keeping things clean and did everything else he was so bad at around the house or didn't have time for. She made him feel so good with the way she was interested in everything he told her and when he held her close to him it felt more than right. Plus, she was loving and supportive of his dreams for what the farm could be. Even though she didn't have a farm background, after they married, she jumped right in and learned how to run the tractor to help him with the field chores or work in the barn.

Teaching her to drive the tractor had been a test of Ben's patience though. She had never driven a standard shift car so the whole clutch and changing gears part was new to her. The handle for the stick shift was right in the middle between her feet and it took strong jerking starts and stops before she figured the clutch to gas timing sequence. Ben thought she'd send him flying a couple of times or give him whiplash as he stood on the hitch clutching the back of the tractor seat while coaching her. Once she got the hang of it though she loved it and felt powerful wheeling such a big piece of equipment around. She just didn't quite estimate the width of the big machine exactly right one day when she took off a piece of the barn door while putting it away. She found other ways she could help with Ben's workload too. She broke open the bales and put hay in front of the cows while he milked and afterward made a good breakfast for them both. He couldn't have asked for a better partner.

Karen thought Ben looked as if he worked out all the time. His body was lean, muscular and tanned. He had dark hair with blue eyes which changed to blue-grey at times. Karen loved the way he looked and how good he smelled when she was close to him. She admired how hard he worked to keep the farm going and didn't give up when things got difficult. When he had told her of his dreams of carrying on his Dad's dairy, they became her dreams too, and she wanted to be by his side to help make them happen. She loved his strong family values and that he thought a wife was meant to be a lifetime partner. He also wanted to be a father someday and wanted to raise children on the farm where they could play outside without fear and learn about nature, working hard and caring for animals. She felt he would make a good father and do everything he could to provide for her, and she loved the way he made her feel protected and sexy.

It was so great too, Karen positively saw his vision, made him believe it could happen, and wanted the same thing for both of them. When this batch of cows had their calves, he could start milking them. Then he'd get them and more of his herd bred again and in one or two years he'd double the stock he had. His sister Amy had married his friend and hunting buddy Warren and they lived 30 miles away. Ben's Dad, before he died, and Warren had purchased a prize bull for a hefty price which came from championship bloodlines. The bull had started life as a 4H project and was used to being handled and being around people but they never let their guard down around him. Bulls can be dangerous, bulls can kill. It had sired the best milkers in Ben and Warren's herds. When the bull was needed, he stayed at either Ben's or Warren's farm, traveling back and forth in a horse trailer. The joke between them was *Have bull, will travel.*

After their marriage, Ben had been thinking hard about expanding the farm. Up past the pond there was a big section of woods and fields his neighbor owned. It was right next to acres and acres of land owned by a Canadian Timber Company they called the French Tract. When his neighbor decided to quit farming and retire, he decided to sell his house and all the land with it. Ben wanted some of those fields to add to the land he had. The realtor suggested the neighbor divide the real estate into the house and separate parcels of land, which was good news to Ben, he only wanted the land, not the house.

He and Karen looked over their finances to see if there was any way they could buy land. They worked on a financial statement of how he could improve his production and get more income by expanding. They planned on selling off timber if they could purchase the wooded parcel. Ben spoke to a timber company regarding buying the logs. He knew there were many red and black cherry trees in there because Ben had hunted in his neighbor's woods for years. Cherry is one of the northeast's most valuable woods and was sought by many mills. It brought a good sum when it was cut and sold for flooring and quality furniture among other uses. Many importers from China were putting shipping containers right at the mills and paying more than U.S. buyers because the wood was in such demand in Asia. Ben also found out the local Agway needed oats and straw to sell, so he planned on putting in a field of grain on the new land. He wanted to harvest the oats and then sell the straw to them also. If all those plans fell into place, they could pay off a substantial part of the loan quickly. The couple took their financial plan to the bank and were surprised when they got preapproval for a loan up to $60,000 to bid on a few of the acres being sold when the auction took place.

Auction day came. Ben eagerly held up his number card when the parcel came up that he wanted. Again, and again the price went up and he kept raising his card, but Ben was eventually outbid by someone he didn't know across the crowd. When another parcel of the land came up that was adjacent to his, he bid on that also, but he was outbid another time by the person with the same card number as before. He didn't get to buy any of the property he wanted. To his surprise, Blair Coleman, a local businessman unknown to Ben, bought every parcel plus the dwellings and said he planned to leave the house vacant. He told the auctioneer and the others who were hoping to purchase land he might rent out the house sometime in the future but not now. He apologized for taking it all but said he wanted to put a nice hunting cabin up back in the woods for him and his buddies to hunt and go four-wheeling. So, Ben was blocked along his neighbor's side of his property from adding any acres to his farm.

Soon after the sale of the land and house, a big yellow dozer came in and cut a dirt roadway back up over the hill and into the woods right through the middle of one of the best fields his former neighbor had worked. Then large dump trucks carrying loads of stone arrived dumping load after load onto the new roadway and spreading the crushed stones out. Soon a big well drilling rig drove back in there, so they could have water at the cabin Mr. Coleman was building. On several days an old Water truck with a green cab and white tank showed up and sprayed volumes of water on the dirt and gravel road to keep the dust down from the construction traffic. They must have had a problem hitting a good pocket of well water because the drilling rig was back in there for a long time. Ben and Karen could hear the thud thud pounding as the drilling continued for days and days. It was going to be a very deep well, but there were areas around those hills much dryer than others or sometimes they hit thick layers of rock to go through with the drill, so it didn't seem unusual the driller was taking so long to get water.

Ben told Karen "It's a good thing our new neighbor is rich, his well is going to cost him a fortune."

After the well-driller was finally done and the pounding stopped, concrete trucks traveled up the new gravel road and soon lumber trucks making deliveries traveled back into the woods and workmen in pickups drove back and forth also. Every day there was traffic up into the building site. Both he and Karen were getting curious about what Blair Coleman's cabin was going to look like. They couldn't see it from their farm because it was over the hill, back in the woods out of sight.

Ben had always hunted deer and rabbit in those woods and fields before with his old neighbor's permission. When he called and asked Mr. Coleman if he could continue to hunt there, he apologized and said: "No, I'm sorry I can't let you do that." He told Ben he and his friends were going to be four-wheeling up there a lot, and he didn't want anybody shooting around them.

Ben then asked him if he would consider allowing him to rent his fields for crops or to cut hay and Coleman didn't care for that idea either. Coleman said he'd rather let them go fallow and grow up into brush and trees, so he'd have more game around such as pheasants, rabbit, and deer to shoot for him and his hunting buddies.

Ben was disappointed, he was familiar with those woods and where he could find turkey and deer hanging out. He had a special spot by a spring back in there where he often sat on a log surrounded by hemlock trees. The game walked within his sights to drink at the spring. He and Warren had taken a buck every year by that spring. They even shared the venison with the former neighbor who had owned those woods before he retired for letting Ben and Warren hunt there. The old gentleman had hunted in those woods for years himself but was too elderly to do it in recent years, so Ben had helped him out by getting his venison for him too.

Soon after Ben had talked to Coleman on the phone, big fences and locked gates were put up around most of the property. Signs were put up with bold red letters on the big gate and all along the fence. They spelled out WARNING KEEP OUT Absolutely No Trespassing for Any Reason. Violators Will Be Prosecuted and Jailed. KEEP OUT. His new neighbor wasn't going to be very neighborly Ben realized.

He must have had a lot of work done because trucks were often going in and out, some even late at night. It was a strange sight to see the headlights of a truck going up the gravel road and disappear into the woods in the dark. Again, Ben thought Coleman was spending a lot to build a hunting cabin for him and his friends and it must be a showoff place for him to impress them.

Fall came around and Ben was looking forward to going hunting with his brother-in-law Warren and hoping to get a buck for each of them as they did every year, however, this year had to be different. Blair Coleman now owned their favorite hunting grounds. The two had walked all over Ben's own wooded acreage for three days looking for deer. They only found old tracks and places where deer had rubbed the bark off tree saplings with their antlers and left scat.

It was quiet over on Coleman's property now, most of the construction must have been done because trucks only came in once and a while now. They were sitting on a log, discouraged by their lack of hunting success when they decided to stop wasting time and risk hunting where they were sure they'd find deer, right back at the familiar spring in the woods on Coleman's land.

"We can be in there and gone with our buck and Coleman will never know. Besides, I'm curious to see what the hell sort of fancy cabin he put back in there anyways," Ben said to Warren. "He's probably got an awesome man cave up there."

"Could be," Warren said. "Only way to find out is to look." Both full of curiosity, they stood up together and headed towards his woods.

The Coleman property was so big it hadn't all been fenced off, so they hiked the back way up over Ben's property and headed towards Coleman's cabin where there was no fence. Warren, as usual, chatted away the whole time, mostly concerning hunting. He was quiet for a short time panting for breath from the hiking and Ben thought, good he's finally taking a breath or run out of things to say, but then Warren spoke up and said, "Hey

Ben, did you hear about the lady who called into one of those talk shows and asked the guy how do the deer know they are supposed to cross at the deer crossing signs?"

"You're kidding me, aren't you?" Ben asked.

"No, she actually did. The DJ at the station told her the Mama Doe teaches little Bambi how to cross the road when it still has its spots, so it knows how to do it when it's older and she believed him!" They both laughed.

"Yeah, I've known a few girls similar to her." Ben said, "Thank God I met Karen."

They reached a place where the new cabin was in view from a distance. It was only a basic square building and not even a very big one either. It wasn't anything like the hunting cabin Coleman had implied he was putting in there to have fun with his friends.

"What the hell?" Warren said, loudly. "It's only a simple building. Certainly, nothing to be bragging as I heard Blair Coleman has been doing in town. Maybe he's got a lot of neat stuff inside it. Boy, can he stretch the truth though. I wonder how wild his fish stories are. He probably tells everyone he landed a great white shark one time."

The two hunters didn't go in close to the cabin. They looked around the woods where they usually hunted and didn't find deer there, but on the way back off the Coleman property they spotted a nice buck just as they were crossing back over to Ben's acreage. Warren got a good clean shot at him and the deer was quickly down and dead. They dressed the carcass and were pleased they got their venison to haul back home. So, finally, after four days of hunting and tramping all over the woods and fields, they were successful. Ben told Karen what he had seen on the Coleman property and she thought Blair Coleman was only puffing himself up with importance regarding what he had built up there and bragging to everyone to make himself look good. They put his cabin out of their thoughts.

The young farm couple had a good autumn. They had venison and beef in the freezer along with vegetables from the garden and the herd was all healthy. Warren brought Lightning the bull over in the horse trailer to spend time with the cows to get them bred. They were very careful about handling him. Lightning had been raised by a 4H kid for the first couple years of his life and was used to people and handling, but bulls can get mean and be aggressive and unpredictable. Lightning had been carted back and forth, loaded and unloaded so much he was used to it and was sometimes cranky but generally was cooperative. Ben and Warren were always careful and alert around him though. Karen asked one time when they were putting him in the pasture with the cows why they called him Lightning.

Warren was quick to reply, "Because he's charged up, hot, and strikes fast." She blushed at his answer. Then he added, "Or how about he hits in a flash and leaves the bovines smiling". He added with a huge grin.

Then Warren turned to Ben and asked. "Hey, did I ever tell you what the Young Bull said to the Old Bull?"

"No, and I'm not going to ask." Ben said, "But I know you'll tell us anyways."

"The young bull was up on the hill and said look at all those good-looking heifers down there in the pasture. Hey, how about we run down this hill and jump on one of them?" The Old Bull answered him slowly saying "Well how about we walk down the hill and jump on them all?"

Ben cringed and said, "Okay, okay, Warren enough with the bull jokes." They were going to switch over to using an artificial insemination service one of these days and retire Lightning, but for now, they were still using the bull they had invested so much money in because he got the job done.

So, it was with hopes and anticipation of growing his dream that Ben and Karen awaited the batch of calves due to be born in the spring. Karen had never seen the birth of a calf and was looking forward to it. Ben's herd was made up of black and white Holsteins, famous for being good milkers. Karen even had names picked out ahead of time. She'd name the first calf Oreo if it was a bull and Moonpie if it was a heifer. When the rest of the cows freshened, she'd wing it and name them one at a time. It was such an exciting time waiting for the new calves. It would be the beginning of a new chapter on the farm with Ben being the caretaker of his parent's dreams and having a new partner at his side.

Chapter Two

WINTER PASSED on Hillside Farm with days of frigid, windy and snowy weather under gloomy grey skies that alternated with days of brilliant sunshine bouncing off a snowy landscape under clear blue skies. Finally, Spring arrived, and it was time for new growth and new life on the farm. Beauty was a large boned Holstein, one of Ben's favorite cows he had chosen to keep instead of selling off. She had already given birth to two calves in previous years and was due to have another any day now. Ben had named her Beauty because she was a perfect example of what a Holstein should look like with crisp-edged black and white patterns on her body, a straight backbone, and an ample udder. She had been restless all day, so Ben put her in a clean stall by herself, spread fresh hay bedding around on the floor then he and Karen kept an eye on her. They could tell the calf was being very active by the bumps pushing out Beauty's sides once and awhile. The cow tried to lie down and then got right back up after a short while, moved someplace else, act as if she was pushing, and do the same thing over again. She couldn't seem to get comfortable.

Finally, she stood up, bellowed loudly and started pushing hard. The front feet came out first, soon they could see a nose and head, and with a tremendous push, the cow dropped the calf behind her in the clean hay. Beauty quickly turned around to see her new calf. Ben jumped into the stall, wiped the calf's nose off and rubbed its ribs to stimulate it. The calf raised its head and made a loud bleating noise.

"It's a heifer, she looks perfect," Ben told Karen, who clapped her hands and jumped with joy. "Look how pretty it is. Oh, Ben, we're parents," she said, grinning from ear to ear.

He laughed shaking his head no and said: "Karen, the cow and the bull are parents, we're just their keepers."

Beauty was watching everything Ben did closely. He pushed the calf in the direction of the cow's udder, so it could get the colostrum, its first food. He explained to Karen, it was very important because it had immunities in it plus, a digestive bacterium to help the calf get off to a good start. The wobbly legged calf looked cute as she started to nurse on the cow. It was butting its head against the cow's udder.

"Ouch, doesn't it hurt the cow, why is it doing that?" Karen asked.

"No, butting doesn't hurt her, it stimulates the cow to let down her milk. It's okay." Ben told her.

They watched the pair as the mother cow and her newborn were bonding. Suddenly, it was acting strange. The calf had milk bubbling out of its nose, wasn't swallowing right and was choking. Ben was concerned and went right to it. He watched the calf stop for a minute then try to nurse again. The same thing happened, it made a choking sound and bubbling milk came out of its nose. Was this a sort of a calf hiccup or what he wondered. If the calf couldn't swallow right to get nourishment, she'd starve. If the calf kept choking and got milk into its lungs, congestion and then pneumonia would set in. Being so small it wouldn't survive. Either way, he felt the outcome was gloomy and disappointing.

Beauty mooed loudly and didn't like it when Ben took the calf away from her. Ben thought perhaps the calf just needed a few minutes break to get its suckling rhythm right.

Karen noticed the look of concern on Ben's face and asked, "what's wrong?"

He shrugged his shoulders and said, "Not sure Hon . . . she's not starting out right." He waited a few minutes and put the calf back onto the cow and the same thing happened, foamy milk was bubbling from its nostrils and it was choking. He took it away again. "We'll try this again in the morning," he said, "after the calf has rested awhile." Ben took the calf to a different penned area separated from Beauty and it agitated her, she mooed loudly in protest at Ben. She stretched her head out over the boards of her stall trying to see her calf. Ben didn't want to separate them but thought it was the best thing for the calf. He had a bad feeling concerning this new calf but didn't want to alarm Karen.

Ben didn't sleep well during the night and as soon as dawn arrived, he headed for the barn to check on the calf. It was not looking good. Already Ben could hear a rattling in its chest and it seemed weak. They can turn so fast and be gone the next moment, he said to himself as he examined the calf, patted its head and stroked its neck. It was a pretty little thing just as Karen had said. He tried putting the calf back with Beauty, but it had the same trouble nursing. Next, he tried feeding it with a nipple pail that had Beauty's milk in it and the same thing happened, foamy milk came out of its nose. He hated to run up a vet bill, even so, this was beyond his knowledge and he needed to get professional help.

He called Doc Morris, the same vet his Dad had used, and he came right out. The old vet had been taking care of the local animals for many years and was liked as well as trusted by the farmers around. He had just about seen and treated everything in his years of practice. He'd even take payment in beef or pork if you were short on cash.

Doc Morris examined the calf after watching it try to nurse and saw it had serious problems right away. "This ain't good." He said to Ben. He stuck two of his fingers in its mouth and the calf started sucking on them. He checked its mouth and throat with a flashlight and couldn't find anything wrong. He listened to its lungs with a stethoscope and told Ben he was already hearing rattling in the calf's lungs.

The old vet stood up and rubbed his chin as he stared at the calf. "Ben this calf is aspirating its milk, and I don't know why. I can't see anything wrong here." He said. "I think it's best to keep it away from Beauty right now. I'm going to give it some nourishment with a tube feeding, also vitamin shots and antibiotics, otherwise there wasn't much we can do, but you can't keep sticking a tube down its throat to feed it every day.

You'll have to wait and see how it's doing tomorrow. You'll know by then if it's going to flourish or falter." He shook Ben's hand, patted him on the back and said, "Let me know what happens." The vet hopped into his road-weary old jeep, waved goodbye and was on his way to another call. Ben checked the calf later and it looked as if it was resting.

The next morning the calf lay on its side, its breathing was labored, and it was so weak it couldn't hold up its head. Later in the day, it died. Karen took it very hard, this farm life with animals was a new thing to her. She hadn't been raised on a farm like Ben who had experience with animals passing before, and she cried hard after seeing the perfect little heifer lying there so still.

"But why Ben? How could something so perfect looking die so soon after being born?" Karen sobbed. Ben pulled her to him and hugged her close trying to comfort her. He remembered how hard he had taken the loss of an animal before.

"Not a good start to building up our dairy Hon," he said, "There will be more calves soon. This happens sometimes, Karen. It's hard to get used to, but it's a part of dairy life." He'd seen calves die had an illness like scours, but not as this one did who looked so perfect and then choked on its first swallows of milk. He wished he knew why at least the cow could give them milk for ten months or more now. Ben would get her bred again, then dry her up for a couple of months before her next calf was born and then she would be making milk again. Hopefully, she'd have a healthy calf within a year. Besides, they had eight more cows freshening in the next few weeks. He'd still be able to increase his herd.

It didn't happen though. Seven of the next calves born during spring had the same problem. They couldn't drink without foamy milk coming out of their nostrils and choking them. They got pneumonia and despite all the different things that Doc Morris and Ben tried to save them, they died. Doc Morris always came right away and when the second one got into trouble with not swallowing right and rattling in its lungs, he was just as worried as Ben about what was happening and wanted to know why. He told Ben "You can take it over to the Veterinary College to see if they can save it. It'd probably cost you well over $2,000 or more; I know one farmer they charged almost $5,000, they weren't cheap, but they have computerized equipment they use to feed and monitor sick animals 24 hours a day and give them meds. But there's no guarantee it will live." It was way over the amount Ben felt he could manage for one calf, so they waited and watched the second one, and unhappily it died also and then a third one and almost all the others too.

Only one heifer in the whole bunch of calves due to be born survived. Karen named the special calf Loner. Doc Morris did a necropsy on two of them and told Ben physically the calves were perfect and should have lived. Ben was devastated, this hadn't happened before, and he couldn't understand what could be wrong. Those same cows had dropped good healthy calves before. Some had grown, been bred and he was milking them now. Why did almost this whole group of calves born this spring die the same cruel, mysterious way?

Doc Morris was at a loss for answers too. He said he'd never seen anything like it before. They started examining everything on the farm. Ben had hired a man to whitewash the inside of the milking area in the barn earlier in the spring. It was only white paint made of lime and water sprayed on the stone and wood walls downstairs. Farmers had been using whitewash for decades to clean and sanitize their milking parlors and it wasn't something harmful. They investigated genetics as a possibility but ruled it out because Warren was using the same bull to sire the cows he had on his farm and all his spring calves were perfectly fine and thriving. They checked the feed Ben was using to find out if it had gotten contaminated somehow with pesticides to keep bugs and mice out of it. If a pregnant cow consumed pesticides it could have affected the calves. Doc Morris told him he knew a Professor Herrick from Rotary Club who was head of the Science Department at Valley View Community College. He thought he could get him to do the testing for free. He did run tests for Ben and the Vet, but Herrick found nothing wrong with the feed or anything else.

Next, they investigated the forage the cows were eating in the pasture. Were there any plants out there such as Nightshade with its red berries that the cows could be eating to cause this they wondered? Together they walked over every area of the pastures and carefully kept their eyes open for anything unusual, nothing was found there either. Ben wasn't using any fly spray or another insecticide on or near the cows, so they ruled spray out too. Doc Morris asked if the cows could have eaten any fruit such as green apples or other fruit which could ferment in one of their four stomachs and cause problems. Ben told him they didn't have access to his orchard or fallen apples. The Doc also asked if Ben was using any weed killers in his cornfield to keep the corn borers away and Ben answered: "No, I stay away from insecticides and herbicides and all of those types of chemicals too."

Finally, they tested the water on the farm. Ben waited weeks for the results from Professor Herrick the head of the Valley View Science Department. He didn't want to find out there was a problem with his water, but he wanted to finally get answers at the same time as to why his calves were born looking perfect then soon died. When the mail came, he read the results from Professor Herrick which stated *No harmful bacteria or algae in the water which could cause illness or harm to livestock. All samples tested were normal and showed no reason to cause illness in cattle.*

After extensive time and investigation Ben still had no answers. They had tested everything they could think of, he just had to put it behind him. It was just one of those spells of bad luck farmer's get, such as when a whole crop fails, or an expensive piece of machinery breaks down and you must shell out lots of dollars to get it fixed. Bad luck happens to everyone. He knew God wasn't up there with a big flyswatter whacking him. He needed to continue working hard and move forward. The loss stayed with Ben though and haunted him at times. He only had one surviving new calf to build his herd back up and those other spring calves had died such a mysterious death.

He couldn't dwell on it or waste any more time, there was plowing and disking, planting and green forage to cut. It was almost time for the first cutting of hay and always upkeep on the equipment to do. Then a few weeks later the second cutting of hay and chopping corn, milking two times a day every day, and the workload continues. Karen needed him to do some repairs on the old white farmhouse too. The eave troughs were coming off on one side of the roof, the bathroom faucet leaked and other odds and ends of repairs needed doing. Karen was patiently waiting for him to get repairs done, nonetheless, he wanted to do what she asked, when she asked him, and not keep putting the house repairs off. She was so helpful to him, he wanted to be helpful to her, he loved her so much.

Chapter Three

FOR WEEKS Ben threw himself into the demands of his work getting up early and staying in the barn or fields late. Karen knew Ben took the loss of the calves and not being able to build his herd up that year very hard. She did too and understood him keeping busy while he got over it, but she missed his company and him talking to her.

He came back into the house one evening after chores and told Karen "Grab your sweater, Hon, I want to show you something, let's go for a walk." They walked up the dug road to the upper pasture and fields, past the small apple orchard with its old heritage trees of Northern Spy and McIntosh. Ben and his sister Amy had picked apples there each September and stuffed them into burlap bags when they were younger. His mom made applesauce plus pies and the bruised apples were turned into cider. Even when the cider turned to vinegar it was still usable. There was one special tree with a low, wide limb protruding out that they used to sit on and pretend it was their horse. They spent many summer holidays playing Robinson Crusoe or Hide and Seek among the trees when chores were done.

A cheerful bobolink was singing his jazzy tumble of notes as he perched on one of the weathered gray fence posts that held up the barbed wire fence along the dug road. The wind was moving the grass gently and bringing them the scent of timothy hay and wild strawberries. Tippy their farm dog, ran ahead of them and was wandering off the dirt and stone roadway zigzagging left and right as he explored the edges of the field. Tippy was a Heinz 57 mix, but mostly Border Collie with a stocky black body, white feet and white tip on his tail. Ben, Karen, and the dog were startled by a booming noise when a pheasant near them burst into the air, flew a short distance away and disappeared into the tall grass of the field.

"Oh boy, he's going to have fun now," Ben said as Tippy barked and took off to chase the pheasant and start playing a game of hide and seek. Tippy was loving it. Ben wasn't worried the dog would get lost running off by himself. Tippy knew these fields and woods along with the way home as well as Ben. "He'll never catch it, Ben told Karen, although he'll have fun trying for quite a while."

They walked up over the hill past the farm's hayfields and hedgerows full of chokecherry and wild scrub apples to where the land leveled back out. There, a small pond at the edge of the grassy pasture shone with the golden red colors of the sun setting in the west. Ben used the land up there to grow corn in one spot and pasture the cows in another field when the other pastures were grazed low. They stopped walking and turned around to look back at where they had been. There were no buildings in sight, only pastures, fields, and woods surrounding them. The sun was setting with a warm western glow, it was going to be a full moon night, so they were in no hurry to get back, they'd have enough light to see the way back to the farmhouse. Down below their herd was lying in the pasture with their front feet folded in under their chests and their jaws moving back and forth as they chewed their cuds.

The fields looked as if a many-hued, green afghan had been spread out covering them. The corn Ben had planted resembled rows of bright green knitted stitches curving here and there where he had pulled the mechanical corn planter with the tractor across the field. The whole valley was laid out before them with Sugar Creek running through it. Now, its slow-moving water was reflecting the golden red colors from the sunset too.

"Sometimes when I'm up here Karen I feel as if I'm the only one on earth. I've worked these fields so much I know the depth of their skin. Ben pointed to the cornfield. Over there I run into a big patch of flat stones and heavy clay soil every spring when I plow. Those rocks must come from middle earth. I always wonder if the corn is going to grow there, yet it does. On the other side, the soil is so loose and fertile it's a pleasure to plow and work it. Can you see those old stumps bordering the field?"

He pointed to a row of massive grey weathered stumps from old trees cut many decades ago. The gnarly stumps were lying tipped up on their sides with their roots pointing into the air looking like a hand with the fingers spread wide open. "That's where a farmer long before me and my Dad pulled stumps out of here to make a field and then lined them up in a row to keep the stock in or make a border for the field. The stumps are called Ghost wood because our ancestors, maybe even a hundred years ago, made those hedgerows by cutting down the trees and digging around those stumps. They used a pick and shovel and prybar along with lots of digging to free them from the earth. Then they hooked a chain onto them and used a horse to pull them out and drag them to the edges for the fence. It must have been backbreaking work. They are well over a hundred years old and when you look at the Ghostwood stumps you get an idea of how huge those trees must have been back then. We don't have huge old growth trees like those anymore. All of Pennsylvania has been logged off at one time. Wild blackberries grow over there, and Amy and I helped Mom pick them in August. She made blackberry jelly and warm berry cobbler and served it with vanilla ice cream made from our own cow's milk. It was so good." Ben's voice trailed off remembering those other times.

"Ben, we can pick blackberries when they're ripe and I'll make cobbler for you." Ben had his arm around her shoulder and he hugged her and kissed her on her forehead. "Sounds great to me." He said. She was always doing something thoughtful for him.

"Those stone walls over there were made to hold the stock in too and mark the boundaries of a farmer's land from his neighbors." He pointed off into the distance where flat stones were piled into meandering walls close to three feet high. "The rocks are from the fields the farmer was plowing long ago. Just imagine the time it took for each one of those rocks to be dug out of the dirt, loaded on a stone bolt then dragged from the field and put into piles. Sometimes an itinerant stone wall builder came around, used the stones off the pile and did the hard job of building the stone wall for room and board and a small fee. They were craftsmen and built a strong, long-standing beautiful wall. It could take weeks and weeks to build a winding wall that would stand solid and intact over all different types of terrain and withstand the force of frost heaving it upwards in the springtime. It makes me angry when some stranger from New Jersey comes out to the country and talks a farmer into selling his stone walls, so they can use them in a ritzy cul-de-sac in the suburbs. Those walls are part of our history, it's our heritage from our farming ancestors and should stay where they were put, on the land they came from. Every one of those stones was touched by a farmer's hand or a stone wall builder many, many years ago."

Ben paused for a moment, looking around. "Karen, it's as if this is all mine and yet it's not mine, you know what I mean? I want to take care of this farm and pass it on to our children if I can." Karen squeezed his hand. Ben continued "It belongs to me and all the other things living and growing and dying here, the grass, the crops, the animals, the trees, the birds, all of it and us too. It's made of the earth and supports all our lives here and it belongs to the earth, we're just caretakers for a while."

"It's so peaceful here Ben, no cars, no planes, no noises," Karen said. Just then a cow mooed loudly below. "Well, except for the cows," she added laughing. The cow bellowed again even louder and longer this time. "Why is she doing that Ben? Is she hurt?"

"No, she's just lovesick Karen and wants the bull to visit her to uh, shall we say get it on. Cows can get really loud and moo a lot when they want some romance. She's singing her cow love song."

"You're kidding me, aren't you?" She asked Ben.

"No, that's what she's really doing." He answered and laughed.

They stood together side by side for some moments, still looking at the rural scene around them. A red fox emerged from the woods near them. It was a beautiful, healthy looking animal with bright rusty red colored fur. The edges of its big ears were lined with black, and it had a white chest and big fluffy tail with a wide band of white fur near the end then changing to black at its tip.

Ben could tell Karen was getting tense. "He won't hurt you, Karen, he's only looking for field mice." They watched as the fox poked his nose into the growing green hay here and there. He must have gotten their scent on the wind because he raised his head, looked curiously their way, and then turned and ran silently off. Ben was glad Tippy was still playing cat and mouse with the pheasant or he'd be chasing this fox most of the night.

"Come on, let's go sit by the pond." Ben took her hand and led her over towards it. They found a grassy spot on the bank and Karen sat down, wrapped her arms around her knees and rested her chin on them.

Ben was next to her with his legs stretched straight out and his ankles crossed. A frog jumped off the bank, caught a bug and landed in the water with a loud splashing noise. Ben leaned back on one arm. "I always forget my problems when I come up here, I can breathe deeply. He took in a long breath and let it slowly out, feeling very relaxed. He picked up a pebble and tossed it into the water and they watched as the circles got wider and wider and before flattening out to nothing. Karen noticed large bubbles coming to the surface and bursting. "It looks like the water is burping." Karen joked, "What's making that happen?"

"There must be a frog or turtle down there letting air out, but gosh I don't know. Haven't seen it happen too much," he told Karen.

Dragonflies with jeweled colored bodies resembled small helicopters hovering over the water of the pond or they were flying low across the surface as if coming in for a landing and then changed their minds and suddenly turn away. One landed on a reed near Karen and she was awed at the delicate lacework lines on its dual wings, its big bulging eyes, and its gleaming, metallic looking, turquoise body.

"Oh, it's so beautiful for a bug," she said, looking at it closely. Karen didn't care for bugs. She had told Ben before, "The only thing worse than a bug is a snake." She thought this bug was quite lovely though.

"Do they bite Ben?" She asked.

"No, Dragonflies eat mosquitos and gnats not us," he said quietly. "They all have their place, they're all important Karen."

"I know Ben, I love nature and wild things the same as you do, but I just can't stand snakes." She shivered at the thought of them and they both laughed. Ben remembered when Karen was surprised by a garter snake in the garden and had frantically called him to kill it. He told her it was harmless, but she retreated to the porch and insisted he kill it to make sure it didn't come back. She didn't want to be surprised by a snake lurking in her vegetable patch.

Karen picked a daisy growing by her and started pulling off the petals one at a time. "He loves me, he loves me not, he loves me, he loves me not, he . . ."

Ben suddenly wrapped his arms around her, and they went over backward onto the grass. "Okay, okay I love you, I love you, I love you," he said kissing her again and again.

Karen laughed, held his face in her hands and getting serious told him. "Ben, I love you so much too and I love this farm and this life. We're going to make it together, don't worry so much, we'll be alright."

They sat back up and were silent for a while enjoying the quiet and each other's company lost in their thoughts.

Ben told her "Yes, we'll just have to ride the float."

"The float?" Karen asked confused. "I don't understand what you mean Ben."

"Our float was a big wooden barn door dragged behind a tractor with a chain to help smooth the soil and knock down any rocks sticking up after plowing and planting, so the mower doesn't hit them when the crop is being cut. Usually, the float has weights on it such as heavy stones or cement blocks, but Dad had me and my sister sit on it along with a few concrete blocks to weigh it down. It was a blast to ride the float. Dad would go fast with the old Farmall and whip it around corners and then take off going fast again. It was a carnival ride to us, and we laughed like crazy at going over the bumps or swinging around those corners. We held on tight to the wooden cross braces as it traveled over the bumpy spots. After a few trips around the field, it was almost smooth and relaxing as if floating on a swimming raft. That's what we have to do to get through this calf problem Karen, ride the float and hang on tight until it smooths everything out again." They sat together in the peacefulness of the early evening silently thinking.

"Ben," she asked, "what was it you wanted me to see up here?"

"You have to wait, it will happen soon, it has to get darker babe, be patient if you thought a dragonfly was pretty you haven't seen anything yet," he told her. The sun had disappeared now, and the stars were starting to appear in the dark sky one by one. Karen noticed the reflection of the stars in the mirror of the pond. It looked as if stars had fallen in and were shimmering just beneath the surface of the water and you could reach in and hold them in your hand.

"Oh, Ben look, she said pointing to the water, is that what you wanted me to see?"

"No, it's not Hon, just be patient a little longer." They sat quietly lost in the peacefulness of the evening. Little by little a few twinkling lights started appearing just over the top of the tall grass in the fields. Within a few minutes, the darkness was lit with tiny blinking lights dancing up and down everywhere and blinking off and on over the fields. The fireflies were out at the peak of their mating season and were blinking their small lighted fluorescent bodies in the dark so they could find each other.

"Wow, Ben this is so awesome." was all Karen could say as she looked at the hundreds and hundreds of tiny dancing lights moving low over the fields. One landed close, Ben caught it and showed it to her in his cupped hands. She looked at its small body closely with its abdomen switching its light on and off similar to the rhythm of a beating heart, then Ben gently let it go.

"One-time Amy and I caught some of them and smeared our arms with their bodies to make them glow. Mom was so mad at us for killing them to cover our arms. She said they were a gift of light in the darkness from God and never do it again. We could kill any spiders or flies if they came into the house, but never lightning bugs, they were different, they were special." Karen leaned against Ben and he put his arm around her as they took in the beauty of the small twinkling lights flashing in the darkness. A chilly breeze came up and Karen was getting goosebumps on her arms. She put on her sweater and told Ben it was getting too cold, so they headed back down the dug road to the farmhouse. They walked in the moonlight hand in hand surrounded by the twinkling of the fireflies.

Later in the fall, Warren's son Kasey was getting an award for a science camp he had attended so Ben and Karen joined Warren and Amy for the ceremony that was held at Valley View Community College not far from where they lived. Kasey had made an awesome display for his science project detailing the layers of soil, rocks, and minerals in the area. He'd made a cutaway model of a hillside to show the different layers of topsoil, subsoil, rocks and water table. He even mixed up epoxy and colored it light blue to show the aquifer deep within the earth. He had various soil screens set up to show how each layer had different sized particles and materials in it. He'd spent hours drawing large colorful diagrams with markers and making handouts too. He visual display exceeded the other students' efforts. He was being recognized for his work along with several other students who had taken a Junior Science Camp during the summer at the college.

The head of the Science Department, Professor Herrick, was the Master of Ceremonies and when Ben saw his name on the program, he recognized it as the person Doc Morris had taken his water and other samples to. Kasey was so excited to get his award when they called him to the stage, he rushed forward and almost tripped and fell on the stage steps. He took big strides across the platform, then quickly shook hands with Professor Herrick with an almost comical pumping motion.

Warren had instructed him "Now when you shake hands with the guy giving you your award don't be afraid to have a good grip, I don't want you shaking hands like a girly."

When Kasey walked away smiling, award in hand, the professor waved his own hand back and forth at the audience as if he had been squeezed by a vice and said: "Wow, that kids got a grip." After the last award was handed out, Professor Herrick said "I want to take a moment to thank our local businessman Blair Coleman for his generous donations to this Junior Scientist Camp and to our Science Department here at the College also. Without his donations and support, we couldn't offer this camp each summer." Then he said, "Mr. Blair Coleman, I know you are here, please stand up."

Having been asked to do so, Mr. Coleman stood up and Ben, Karen, and Warren turned around to see what he looked like as the audience was applauding. Blair was dressed impeccably, with an expensive suit and tie. His dark hair was thinning on top and he was combing it over to cover a bald area. He was a short, stocky man with a shirt that stretched the buttons to the limit to cover his bulging belly. He turned and waved identical to a politician at the applauding audience and then back at Professor Herrick before quickly sitting back down.

Warren leaned over to them and said, “No wonder he needs a place to use four-wheelers to hunt, he couldn’t hike too far after game with a gut like that.”

“Shh . . .” Karen frowned and warned him to be quiet. Ben had only seen Coleman briefly at the farm auction and wanted to introduce himself and Karen to him as his neighbors. They thought they could do so after the ceremony, however, the crush of the crowd letting out was too much to notice where he had gone, and they missed him. They headed on over to the Frosty Scoop to get ice cream to celebrate and Kasey showed everyone his Certificate of Accomplishment. His eyes got big when he opened the envelope it was in and pulled out a $20 bill.

Warren joked “Guess Kasey’s buying ice cream for all of us tonight.”

Kasey quickly said “Oh, no way, I’m keeping this for myself.” and stuffed it of sight into his pocket.

Warren was full of his stories and talkative as usual. He asked Ben if he heard about the lady who called into the radio station and wanted to know why people must hunt animals for meat? Why can’t everyone go to the supermarket to get it instead? They don’t kill animals and they have lots of meat there. “She must think it’s a manufactured product like plastic. It may be sometime in the future. Hell, I heard they even grew an ear on a mouse's back, anything's possible I guess, but right now meat doesn't come from a test tube, it comes from a cow." They all shook their heads and laughed at how clueless some people could be.

Karen started scratching her arm and Ben asked her "Did you remember to put your cream on?"

"Yes, I did Ben, but it still bothers me." She'd been having trouble for several weeks with sore, itchy and watery rashes breaking out on her arms and legs, even on her back, and the doctor had told her it was contact dermatitis and prescribed a cream to help her. He told her to watch what she used in the laundry and what touched her skin and stay away from perfumes, and similar things. They hadn't figured out what was causing the rash. She changed her soaps, the laundry detergent, stopped using perfumes and tried different kinds of creams, yet the rashes kept coming back. Ben had even stopped using aftershave thinking it might be the problem, but the rashes didn't stop for her. They even joked that she might be allergic to Ben.

He was beginning to wonder if it wasn't an emotional "woman thing," yet he didn't want to say that and possibly hurt her feelings. She was forgetting important things too. They got a late notice from the feed company because she forgot to pay the bill even though they had the money set aside for it, and it wasn't the first time she had forgotten something important. She kept forgetting where she left her keys and she lost track of time a lot. She didn't appear to be under any stress, yet he spent such long hours out of the house working the farm so often he wasn't sure. Did she have too many responsibilities, he wondered? There was so much work to being a farm wife. She seemed happy though and told him often how much she loved being a farmer's wife. But he wondered if she had taken on too much responsibility.

Chapter Four

SPRING CAME around and there was new growth and birth going on all around them. The pastures were lush with bright green new grass and apple, pear and chokecherry trees were covered with white and pink blossoms on their branches. The robins, bluebirds and other birds had come back and there was nesting going on everywhere. Barn Swallows had built mud nests in the corners of the barn and were swooping in and out the open door. Ben's favorite cow Beauty was having walking problems though. She was dragging her right hind leg sometimes, so he had Doc Morris come out to check her health. The Vet thought she had strained a muscle with possible nerve injury there, so he gave Ben medicine for her and told him to wait and see if she walked better in a week or so. A cow needed to move around and get up and down or sickness would set in.

They both anxiously awaited the arrival of the first spring calves to be born that year. The cows had gotten bred by the master of those ceremonies Lightning. Ben was still milking the cows who had given birth to calves last spring and he could do that for a little while longer, but it was almost time to dry them up to let them rest a short while before they calved again. He had some heifers due to drop calves for the first time this spring, so he was looking forward to having more milkers. It wasn't long before one of them started showing signs of giving birth soon and Ben anxiously monitored her as she started laboring. Once again, he set up a clean stall for the cow with fresh hay bedding. Calves could be born in the pasture, but he liked to keep an eye on the cow when she was going to give birth just in case there was a problem and she or the calf needed his help. He had a calf born one time with a piece of the birth sack over its nose and mouth and when it took its first deep breath in it sucked the sack deep into its throat and suffocated. He didn't want to lose any calves if he could help it.

Ben wasn't calling Karen down to watch the birth of this calf. She had gotten so upset when the other calves died, he didn't want her to go through the sadness again. The cow dropped the calf after a short while of hard pushing, then it turned around and started licking its face and body to clean it off. So far, so good Ben thought. He watched as the calf tried to stand sticking its rear end up first, next the front legs straightened up, and it pushed itself into a standing position.

"It's a bull this time, it could be beef in a couple years, I'll take that." He said to himself. The calf started walking and looked as if it was drunk and taking a sobriety test. Then it got its bearings and made its way right to the cow's udder to drink. It butted the cow to help get the milk down and started sucking on a teat. Ben watched the calf nursing. He waited to see if the nightmare repeated this year. The calf was gulping milk okay at first and Ben relaxed, but then tragically the same thing happened again, foamy milk started coming out of both nostrils and it was choking. Shocked and dismayed, he couldn't believe it was happening again. He jumped into the stall cursing and took the choking calf away from the cow and started thumping on its chest to help it breathe. He realized he had another calf he had to fight to save and he'd probably lose the battle one more time.

"This is too much, he shouted, why the hell is this happening to me?" He felt as if he was being punished for some unknown reason.

In the evening he told Karen they had a new calf, but it had the same problem feeding as the others and they were most likely going to lose it too. He had struggled so much last spring with this problem he didn't have any hope left the calf could get over this and go on to be strong and healthy. Karen tried to comfort him, saying maybe it will be the only one this time, but she had a sick feeling in the pit of her stomach. She couldn't help but worry about the calves yet to be born.

Later in the night as they lay in bed Karen told him, "We'll find out what's happening and fix it, Ben," she said gently, "Things are going to be okay, there's an answer somewhere."

"I sure as hell hope it comes soon," Ben said then snuggled down under the covers.

Karen continued reading the book she had started. Even though she wasn't pregnant she was reading up on how to raise children. She wanted to be a good Mom when the time came. "Ben, this is interesting." She said. "This author writes that nowadays children aren't free to explore and be creative as they used to be. Most of their activities have rules, guidelines or outcomes they are expected to achieve such as in sports or video games. They've lost touch with nature because they can't roam freely and explore the woods and natural places due to the fear of 'stranger danger,' or because they live in developments similar to what I did and don't have a place to do that. Parents are afraid to let them out of their sight to play by themselves, and when they do go outside its usually to a small neighborhood playground with swing sets and no place where they can dig in the dirt, or cut down saplings, move rocks and make discoveries."*

Ben replied, "Who can blame the parents for wanting to keep them close, the way the world is today."

Karen continued, "He also says children really need to make connections with nature. They need to do simple activities such as building a fort out of sticks or creating a fairy or toad house all by themselves. They should be able to take things apart, move them around, investigate and reassemble them into something they think of on their own without someone judging their activity. It stimulates their curiosity about the world, gets them problem-solving and boosts their creativity. He also mentions that letting children get dirty while playing is actually good for them. There's s type of gut flora, I won't read the scientific name, that promotes healthy digestion and it's getting destroyed due to the overuse of antibiotics.

---

* Paraphrased from the book *Last Child in the Woods* by Richard Louv.

Ben told her sleepily "Amy and I used to build dirt mountains for our Matchbox cars. She enjoyed playing with them as much as I did. We had dirt roads and bridges all over our mountain and even made big puddles so our cars could get all muddy driving through them. We had cliffs they could fly off and crash and tunnels they could go through all on that dirt mountain. It was so much fun. We spent hours doing that. Guess that qualifies as playing in the dirt."

Well, scientists now believe a little dirt accidentally consumed now and then can actually help a child." She paused, "Sure puts a new slant on that five-second rule. Wow! I'm so glad our children will be raised on a farm where they can run around and play freely. I guess they will be making mud pies too. I'm not going to taste them though!" She paused to see if Ben was listening. "Ben, did you hear that?" All she heard beside her was a loud snore. He was so tired and worried about the mysterious deaths of the calves; she was glad he had fallen asleep. Karen closed her book, switched off her reading lamp and fell asleep dreaming of patting mud together for pretend cookies with her future child.

Sometime in the night, Ben woke, restless and concerned, not knowing how to stop the loss of the calves. He walked down the hallway stairs to the kitchen and made himself a cup of coffee. As he sat there sipping it and brooding over his problems he looked across at the refrigerator where Karen had posted family pictures and cute sayings. He read a little sign by a comical picture of a farmer on a tractor with the wording *Him and His Farmall are Sexy* and smiled. Then he noticed the rectangular doctor's appointment card for Karen.

They had been trying to have a baby but weren't having any luck, so they were getting help. His eyes lingered onto the picture of his nephew Kasey getting his Science Award last Fall. He paused, looking at it and remembered the ceremony and Professor Herrick's words afterward, *and we want to thank Blair Coleman for his generous donations to our Science Department.* Something concerning those words didn't sit right with him, yet he wasn't sure why.

His dog Tippy padded into the kitchen, sat down by Ben and rested his head onto Ben's knee.

"You've been on this farm a long time too, haven't you fella?" He said to the old dog while stroking the soft fur on his head. Tippy looked up at him with his big black eyes. "I'm trying to keep us going Tippy, but it's getting tough, so tough." The dog seemed to understand what he was saying and gave a slight whimper.

"I remember when you were only a pup and Dad brought you home to me. It was a few years ago, wasn't it?"

Ben noticed the pile of bills laying on the counter that still had to be taken care of. Where he was going to get the money for all of them, he didn't know. He had needed the new calves badly to build up the herd for milking income in the future. Now, he was caught between a rock and a hard spot, so they say. Not a big enough check to pay all the bills and not enough income to buy more cows which usually cost from $1,200–$3,000 each for a cow with good milking history. Even if he bought calves which would be cheaper, it'd take 2½ to 3 years before they'd be old enough to have a calf themselves and then be milked. It was a long time with so many bills coming in to only have a small milk check each month. He was in a vicious cycle.

Lately, he was wondering if he should diversify and raise other stock besides having a dairy. He thought he might try raising hogs or flocks of chickens for the producers. They would loan him a little money up front to do that, but it would mean more buildings, equipment, and extra money to get stock and feed. Plus, there was no way he could take on so much more physical work plus run his dairy. There wasn't enough time in each day to do so much.

Ben looked at the one good picture he had of his Dad. It was in a simple frame and hanging on the kitchen wall. His father had hated to have his picture taken and always turned away from the camera or put his hand up to block the shot. He always said, "All pictures ever did was make you feel older when you looked in the mirror."

Ben had snapped the one on the wall when they got the new Farmall tractor and his Dad was using it for the first time. It was a great picture of his Dad smiling and happy with his new red farm toy. Ben's eyes welled up when he saw his Dad's familiar face.

"Dad, I can't figure out what to do." He said and shook his head slowly back and forth. "Karen's got problems with allergies or something, and the cows are in real trouble. I'm having a tough time paying the bills. I wish you were here." His voice trailed off and with a deep sigh and he repeated: "I wish you were here to help me."

There was a photo of Ben on the wall as a young boy with his mother too. They were standing together, and she had her arm around his shoulder. I was probably close to 10 years old in that picture he thought. Right about the time he had learned to drive the tractor himself. He stared at the photo and felt her strength hugging him and telling him whatever happens he can handle it. A calm came over him and he finished his coffee and went back to bed beside a sleeping Karen.

The next morning, he had to run into town for supplies at the hardware store. One of his friends from school was there also. He was a young farmer too and Ben and Doug often talked about their farms when they ran into each other. After they made the usual greetings his friend asked "Hey what's up? I heard you lost calves, what a bummer, what's going on?"

"Yeah, I've been having a bad run of luck lately, you know how it is sometimes in farming. Just can't figure out why I'm losing them. Doug, I ran so many tests and didn't find anything. They choke on the cow's milk as soon as they take their first feeding and can't swallow it right. They can't even swallow calf starter when I give it to them with a nipple pail."

Doug shook his head and said, "Humpt, never heard of calves having swallowing problems, that is a strange one." He paused for a minute, then said "You know, maybe it's one of those damn, weird viruses' mosquitos carry, like the one where the baby's head is way too small. What do they call it, Seeka? No, I think its Zeeka or some damn foreign name like that! Isn't there even one called an Egyptian thing or something now people can get? Your cows could have some foreign thing."

"Do you mean West Nile Virus?" Ben asked.

Doug answered, "I don't know. You can't keep up with all the damn shit going around these days. Anyways, mosquitos could be passing something on to them. It's possible you know. You could even become famous for a new disease your calves have."

"I don't want to be famous; I want to be farming," Ben told him.

Ben thought for a moment about what his friend had said. He hadn't considered mosquitos causing some sort of cow disease. They always did have mosquitos or other biting insects around. Even the evening when he and Karen watched the fireflies at the pond they were getting bitten by mosquitos.

"You know, maybe that is a possibility." He said to his friend. "I'll have to look into it."

Doug shook Ben's hand and said, "Hang in there Ben, everyone's rooting for you." He'd had hard times on his farm too over the years and knew personally how it could weigh you down. Word had gotten around the small town, something unusual was happening at Ben's farm and they wondered if the same thing might happen to them. There were so many odd diseases happening to the animals. Things such as Mad Cow Disease and a wasting disease deer can get in their brains that makes them act crazy. You never know what might show up next. As Ben headed back home he couldn't help wondering if he'd missed something like the mosquitos causing sickness in his herd. An insect passing on a virus of some sort could be the blame for this horrible problem with his calves. It couldn't be making the humans sick though he should have had something happen to him by now. The possibility of a virus wasn't that remote. He decided to collect live mosquitos and take them to a lab over in Mansfield.

After doing his barn chores and getting sweaty, he pulled his sleeve up past his elbow and waited. He was standing in the aisle behind the cows. If there were any disease-carrying mosquitos biting the cows it would be as good a place as any to catch them. It didn't take long before one landed on his arm and started biting him, and then another joined in and another, soon there were several dining on his blood buffet. He quickly put a glass jar over them and trapped them inside. He managed to tip it back up and get the lid on before they escaped.

"Ha, I got you, ya damn vampires!" he said to them holding up the jar and watching them buzz the glass. "Now, we'll find out what you have been up to besides sucking my blood." He quickly put the jar out of sight before Karen got wise to what he had been doing. The next day he drove over to Mansfield and dropped the mosquitos off at EnBioApp, a lab there that specialized in Environmental and Biological Advanced Practices and Procedures and asked them to check the mosquitoes for any viruses or diseases they might carry.

"How soon will you give me the results?" he asked the lab technician.

"We'll give you a call as soon as we know." The lab tech said. "It'll take a few days."

A couple of days later Ben got the call he had been waiting for. EnBioApp told him there was nothing unusual about the mosquito samples. "Only thing there was the blood of some poor animal they had been feeding on." He said.

"Umm . . . that would be me," Ben told him sheepishly.

"We sort of figured out you were the animal when it came up as O positive. Well, even though you volunteered as a test subject, which I don't recommend you ever do again, there are no diseases or viruses in the mosquitos you brought us."

Ben thanked him for the quick work he had done. He told him he'd mail in a check for the fee by the end of the week. He hung up the phone and said to himself, "Still no answer, just another dead end."

Warren called and told him Kasey had a ball game not far from the farm, would he and Karen want to come to the local park, meet up with them and watch him play? It sounded like a fun evening for everyone, so they planned to do that. Kasey was the catcher on his team which was sponsored by the local gravel and stone dealer. The team wore grey shirts, pants with red lettering and were called the Crushers. They were up against the Inky Dinks, a team sponsored by the local printer. Their shirts were tie-dyed with lots of colors and they wore black pants to go with them. It was easy to tell one team from the other.

Sitting on the bleachers, watching those kids having fun while being focused on playing the game was so enjoyable. Ben looked around the stands and saw fathers and mothers cheering for their own kids. Most of them were people he had gone to school with. Occasionally one waved back when they recognized him too.

Ben thought back to when he was in Little League. His Mom and Dad sat on those same bleachers watching him play. Looking around at the signs posted near the scoreboard he recognized familiar businesses in town, the Frosty Scoop, Cliff's Auto, Valley Insurance, he patronized most of those companies, and other business who been in town even when he was a boy. Then he spotted a sign for a business called MetInverse Enterprises, a new one to him.

"Warren, do you know who MetInverse Enterprises is?" Ben asked.

"No, I don't Ben, but they've been donating a lot in this town and has given funds to this ballpark. They're even considering changing the name to MetInverse Park instead of after our old coach. That just ain't right, our coach donated so much of his time here working with these kids!"

Kasey caught a pitch to home base and tagged out a runner before he reached the sack. Warren stood up and yelled, "That's my boy, great job Kasey!" Then he sat back down and told Ben one of these days you'll be here with your own son cheering. Ben wanted a child of his own as much as Karen did, but didn't care if it was a son or a daughter.

Amy was saying "This is so great." As she snapped away taking pictures. "I'm such a proud Momma."

Ben and Karen looked at each other and he said: "Warren, we're certainly trying to have a child."

"Yeah, I'll bet. It's such hot sweaty work, isn't it?" He asked grinning. Amy poked him in the ribs and told him to leave them alone.

Karen had gotten her hopes up only a few weeks earlier when she thought she was pregnant, but it was another false start and she wasn't. They had been to the doctor more than once to find out if something wasn't quite right with either one of them. After doing thorough tests he had told them there was no reason they couldn't get pregnant, there was nothing concerning in the results, everything seemed normal. He said sometimes these things take time, to be patient and don't stress about it. Making a baby for some folks is like anything else new. Sometimes it just takes practice to make it happen.

"Well, we can handle that part," Ben said making Karen blush again.

"Give it more time, then if you are still having trouble conceiving let me know and I'll refer you to a specialist." The doctor had said as he shook hands with the couple. As they walked back out to their pickup Ben told her "Don't worry Hon, the Doc said we're both okay, it will happen soon enough."

Karen answered, "I know Ben, but I want to be pregnant now," as a tear rolled down her cheek.

He wrapped her in his arms and whispered, "We'll keep practicing until we get it right. That's fun, isn't it?" He asked hugging her. They walked quietly to the truck, both wondering how different life was going to be with a child of their own.

Kasey's team the Crushers, won the game 12 to 9. It was a close contest and had been exciting to watch. The players lined up and walked down the row shaking hands with each other. Ben, Karen, Amy, Warren, and Kasey went out for ice cream at the Frosty Scoop afterward to celebrate and go over the highlights of the whole evening. The relaxing time kept both their minds off their troubles for a short while at least.

Chapter Five

BEN STILL didn't have an answer to the mysterious reason his calves were dying after months of trying to find out. He resolved to keep working away hoping something happened, so he had a way to solve the problem.

Karen was learning how to can and preserve the vegetables from their garden. They were picking sweet corn, squash, and tomatoes then sharing them with Warren and his family. She had learned a lot since becoming a farmer's wife. She had learned to bake also, was good at it, and it became one of her favorite things to do. She decided to see if there was a way, she could earn a little income from it. She investigated everything she needed to do to get her kitchen certified so she could sell her baked goods at the local Farmer's Market. There were so many regulations and rules to follow. She arranged to have the kitchen inspection and passed it. Next, she had to master the rules regarding labeling plus packaging the products she made. They gave her specific directions to list the largest ingredients first on down to whatever was included in the smallest amounts in her goods. There had to be a warning included if there were any nuts or dairy products and it had to be in a certain size typeface and wrapped a special way. It was a couple of pages of rules, but she managed to comply with each of them and proudly set up her tables where the market was held in a shady park in town on Saturday's mornings.

She had been baking the whole day before and into most of the evening. It was satisfying to knead the bread and watch it rise and bake it into a golden-brown loaf. She enjoyed making several kinds of cookies too. The house smelled wonderful with all the aromas of the cookies and bread baking. She had to slap Ben's hand lovingly away when he tried to grab a handful of cookies, but he was happy with the imperfect scraps of different cookies he got to munch. Her baked goods were a hit on Saturday, and she sold out before the market was done. She headed home feeling proud having earned a few dollars for bills plus some "mad money" of her own to use for extras or to have a dinner out.

At first, it had seemed as if it was too much work to make and sell the bread and cookies each week, but once she made it past learning how to comply with all the regulations and got organized, it became fun to focus on whatever she wanted to bake weekly. The farm kitchen still had several of the baking sheets and other kitchen items Ben's mother had used including her old cookbook. It had a special meaning to read the handwritten notes on recipes from the mother-in-law she had never met. She even came across the berry cobbler recipe Ben said he had enjoyed so much and made it for him one night.

Karen had several return customers each Saturday but there was one particular senior man she looked forward to seeing each week. He had grey hair, was getting on in age, and usually had a warm smile on his face. He always bought a loaf of her Country Bread, it was a good white loaf for sandwiches or toast, plus six cookies. He'd pick whatever special cookie she was featuring for the week. When she handed him his sack of goodies along with his change, he told her "Young lady I'm in love with you. If I was only 50 years younger, we'd be an item for sure." It was said in good nature; he was such a sweet old gentleman she enjoyed his flattery.

One of her best-selling items was her Cheesecake Brownies with swirls of cream cheese through the moist dark chocolate. Another popular item was her Cinnamon Raisin Bread which sold out quickly each time. After she had been doing the market for a few Saturdays customers arrived early, waiting for her to get set up, so they could grab her products early before she sold out. Ben was so proud of her as a small businesswoman. Besides earning money for herself she got praise for her skills along with having a good time socializing with the other vendors and customers.

Karen's only real concern about selling at the market was the red rash that kept returning. She was uncomfortable with people seeing the breakouts and felt very self-conscious when the blotches appeared on her arms, so she wore long-sleeved shirts to cover them up even on warm, sunny days.

Ben had to run into town during the week to pick up barbed wire to repair the fence. When he returned home, Karen had just gotten out of her bath. She sat in a kitchen chair in her light coral chenille robe with her feet up on the chair opposite her. Ben poured coffee for them while Karen applied a natural herbal cream she traded for at the market to the red rash on her legs.

"I'm noticing more bumps." He told her, "Is it bothering you much?"

"No, but it bothers me, I don't think I look sexy for you with these red patches," Karen replied.

"No problem there," Ben said lovingly while looking deeply into her eyes, he took the jar of cream out of her hands and started gently applying it to her legs. "You're still my red-hot momma." he leaned in close, kissed her and smiled.

"Did you remember to pick up the barbed wire I ordered for you?" she asked him.

"Yes dear, I did . . . boy what a nag." He said teasing her.

They talked about repairing the fence along with the other things they had to accomplish this year. They wanted to take a couple days' vacation also and were hoping Warren and Kasey could do the chores for them while they were gone. They were tossing around different places where they could go. Their favorite day trips were to places where they had colonial villages or historical homes they could tour. They both enjoyed seeing the artifacts from long ago together with learning the history of the people who lived in those places. It had to be a short trip though. Farmers couldn't stay away from their responsibilities for very long.

Karen asked again "Ben did you remember the barbed wire?"

Ben looked at her strangely and said patiently "Karen, I just told you yes, I did."

"Oh, I'm sorry I have been kinda forgetful lately. I guess I don't have my head screwed on right." They both laughed; however, Ben was getting more concerned regarding her being so forgetful.

"Hey, let's have some dessert," Ben told her.

"Sounds good to me, let me get dressed and we'll go out to the Frosty Scoop" she stood up and answered. Ben stopped her before she walked away and put his arms around her while tenderly kissing her neck.

He whispered in her ear. "No Hon, I'm not talking about a food dessert, I've got something even better in mind. Remember the Doc said we only need to keep practicing?" They both laughed. "Oh, that dessert," she said, and they walked smiling, arms around each other's waists, towards the bedroom.

The next day Ben was out repairing the fence when he saw a big truck go back up the road to Coleman's property. He got thinking how Coleman had said he planned to go four-wheeling plus hunting back in there with his buddies, but he hadn't seen any cars or trucks go up the road with any four-wheelers on a trailer, only big trucks. It had been a very long time since Coleman had bought the place surely it must be finished by now. Ben decided it was time to check that cabin out more thoroughly and get in touch with Warren to help him do it. Later in the day, he gave Warren a call.

"Warren, how'd you like to come over tomorrow and do some scouting with me?" Ben asked.

"What's on your mind?" Warren asked.

"I'm curious about this cabin Coleman built, we didn't get close enough before for a good look at it. I want to see more this time. There hasn't been much traffic on his dirt road, now is as good a time as any to be nosey. Can you come over?" Ben asked.

"Sure, I'm up for snooping around anytime, let's go for it. I'll be around tomorrow afternoon, see ya then." Warren said.

The next afternoon Warren showed up to help Ben check out the cabin. When Ben told Karen what they were up to she was worried about them trespassing on the neighbor's property. She reminded them both, of the warning signs he had posted on the gate and fence, plus the strong statements of prosecuting any trespassers if they were caught.

"Yeah, but they won't catch us, Karen. I know my way around those woods, remember it's my old stomping grounds." Ben kissed her, asked her to please keep the coffee hot then he and Warren headed out the door before she had a chance to talk the two out of it. Ben decided they should hike in the way they did before when they were hunting and not up Coleman's dirt road in full view in case anyone did show up to go back to the cabin. Besides, along the front of his property, there was that tall fence to get over and neither one of them wanted to climb that thing. They walked up over Ben's field, into his woods then continued over to Coleman's property where it wasn't fenced. They checked around carefully to be sure no cars or trucks were near the cabin before moving in closer to it. Once they were in front of the building, they checked around and sensing it was clear, they walked up onto the porch. Warren turned the door handle and found it was locked.

"Now what wise guy?" he asked Ben as he pressed his face against the glass window while shielding his eyes to look inside. "Man, this is so sparse even for a hunting cabin. There's hardly nothing in there." Ben walked over to the window to look in also. He only saw a table with papers on it and a few chairs. They could see there was a little galley type kitchen with a counter and cupboards, but not much else.

"I can't see into the other rooms," Warren said. "Wonder what he's got in there? I'm not noticing any comfortable furniture or anything here Ben. What kind of a man cave is this? He's supposed to have lots of money."

"I know what you mean Warren, we'd have a better place than this," Ben told him. Suddenly they heard a big truck coming up the dirt road. They turned, faced each other and both said at the same time "Oh hell!"

"Hurry Warren, we've got to get out of here. Let's get around back so they don't see us, quick."

Immediately they jumped off the porch, ran around to the back of the cabin and fled into the woods. They hid behind thick trees and stands of brush. From their vantage point, they could hear the truck drive past the cabin as well as see it head up near where they were hiding. When it came closer, they noticed it was a tanker truck with a green cab and white body. The word WATER was painted in large black letters on the white sides of the big tank. The sign on the driver's door read Keith Tynor Trucking.

Warren quietly told Ben he had noticed the same truck at the town park filling the pool there where Kasey swam at times. The driver pulled up to a concrete pad, shut the truck off and jumped out of the cab. He was a small, weary-looking older man, with grey stubby whiskers. You could tell he was used to working hard for several years and still did. He wore worn navy-blue work pants with matching shirt and a tattered old baseball cap. He took the cover off the wellhead that was in the middle of a concrete pad and then got a big hose attached to the back of his truck. He stuck the hose down the well, turned on a compressor and started pumping water into the well.

"The wells way up here? Ben asked. "Why is it so far from the cabin?"

"Whoa, what the hell is he doing anyways?" Warren wondered. "Why would he be dumping water down a water well?"

"Damn if I know," Ben said.

Warren wondered "Do you suppose the driller never hit a good supply of water, so he has to bring it in?"

"Don't know." Ben said, "This whole place isn't the hunting camp I thought it was; makes me wonder what Coleman had planned."

They could see the truck driver was finishing off unloading his contents of water then putting things back as they were. He drove his truck back down to the cabin, they heard him shut the motor off, then the sound of the cabin door opening and later closing again. In a few minutes the truck engine started, they heard gears being shifted and it took off back down the hill.

The men left without doing any more snooping before anyone else showed up to find them there. It was disappointing that the cabin turned out to be such a bare, uncomfortable building from what they saw looking in the window after the bragging Coleman had done about building a hunting cabin for himself and his buddies.

"Well his place sucks," Ben said shrugging his shoulders as they walked away. "If I was wealthy, I'd have put up a better cabin."

That got Warren fantasizing, so he said, "I'd have kegs in there along with a big screen TV with satellite hookup for sports and movies. There'd be La-Z-Boy recliners for sure to lounge in, make that vibrating recliners in addition to deer heads with 12-point racks mounted on the wall. We'd need a lock on the door to keep the women out so they weren't snooping when we weren't around, plus security cameras further down the driveway if we were staying there, so we can see them coming ahead of time to lock those doors while we put all the beer cans, cigars, and Playboy magazines, away." They both walked away joking and laughing about what they'd have in their man cave if they had one.

The pair got back to the house a short while later still having fun talking. They filled Karen in on what they had seen at the Coleman cabin as well as telling her that a Water truck came while they were there.

"I know I saw it go up the road, but I had no way to warn you. Ben, are you sure he doesn't have a game camera set up somewhere by the place and has recorded you being there?" She asked him as she poured coffee in addition to setting out cookies for them.

"Whoa," Warren said suddenly serious, "We never thought of that. God, I hope there wasn't one, Ben we could be charged with trespassing for sure. What could our excuse be for being at his cabin if he asks us?"

"I have no idea Warren, but we'll have to come up with something in case he does," Ben told him.

"Well, if it makes you two feel any better, I'll bring both you criminals my cookies in jail," Karen said, but she was worried they had gotten into something they'd have trouble explaining their way out of that day and wondered if the police would be showing up at their door.

CHAPTER SIX

BEN'S FAVORITE cow Beauty was still having problems with that one leg not moving right making her limp badly. He was getting more concerned it may be a permanent injury and not a pulled muscle or something like that. The vet took another look at it and now thought it must be arthritis in her hip this time instead of an injury because it had lasted so long. A pulled muscle should have healed by now, he said. The only thing you could do for her to treat arthritis in a cow was keep her out of the cold, wet weather as much as possible, he told Ben. You can't pump her full of steroids and pain killers and still sell her milk so that was out. Just keep her away from the dampness and don't make her hurry anywhere. It's still okay to milk her along with treating her the same as the rest of the herd.

Ben had Doc Morris check out two more of his cows while he was there that had patches of hair missing on their coats.

"This is probably mites." The vet told him while getting a big bottle of medicinal shampoo from his bag and giving it to him. He told Ben to wash those two cows down with a good soapy solution of it, let it sit for a few minutes and then rinse it back off.

"You mean I have to run a cow wash now?" Ben asked him joking.

"Sure do," the vet said, "and don't forget to rub down the fenders and make sure the horns work. Also, watch out for their exhaust pipe, you never know when crap might fly out of it." He joked right back at him, then getting serious he said "Ben, I haven't seen you in quite a while. Did you ever find out what was going on with those calves? It was a damn shame you are losing so many animals."

"No, I didn't Doc," Ben answered. "It's got to get better now though, we've had our share of troubles, time for good luck to happen now." The old vet agreed with him, packed up his gear to leave, then shook Ben's hand and said "You're still a good farmer Ben. Don't let it get you down."

There were nights it did lay heavy on Ben's mind though, often he couldn't fall asleep thinking about the calves dying within a few days. This night he lay on the bed staring at the ceiling. There had to be a reason, he felt sure of it. His place, Hillside Farm was in northeast Pennsylvania, but there wasn't any fracking for gas drilling going on near him. He never saw any fracking trucks on the roads hauling near their place either, but he checked on it to be sure. After the county officials told him there weren't any gas fracking activities going on or holding ponds for their fracking fluids for many miles around him, that method to get at gas deposits was ruled out as the possible reason for causing his loss of animals. He was quite sure it was an environmental reason though, and not genetic, but what? He decided before he finally fell asleep, he'd run all the tests again, perhaps they just overlooked something.

In the morning he told Karen what he wanted to do and asked if she'd not only go along with, she'd help him also. He wanted to take the samples over to EnBioApp in Mansfield this time the place he had taken the mosquitos to. "It's going to cost us to run the tests we need to do, not free like the Science Department at Valley View was, where Professor Herrick worked, but EnBioApp might find results that were missed earlier." He told her. "I'm sure they will be more thorough with the testing."

"Ben, you know I want answers too," she said. "Let's do it."

"I'm going to get instructions from the lab on what they want me to collect and exactly how to do it. Then we'll get started." Ben told her.

Ben called EnBioApp and they instructed him on how to keep the samples fresh by putting each of them in new Ziploc bags, so they don't get contaminated in any way. They collected cow feed, and samples of hay, they scraped whitewash off the walls of the dairy barn again, they even clipped samples of grass and weeds out of the pasture. Karen cleaned canning jars and got water in a jar from the barn when it was first turned on, then she let the water run for five minutes and collected more in another jar. They hiked up to the pond where the cows drank and got water samples there too. They even included samples of the antiseptic wash they used to clean the cow's udders before they put the milker on them. Everything was labeled, dated and even had the time of day it was collected along with where. They loaded the samples into a cardboard box, drove over to EnBioApp and dropped them off.

"When can I get the results?" Ben asked the lab technician.

"Some of them you'll know right away whether we find anything or not. Other tests can take a while to run, we need to grow cultures, and so forth. We'll get back to you as soon as possible. Have you got everything labeled with the date they were collected including your name and number, so we can contact you?"

"Yes, it's all there," Ben said, "I followed your directions on how to do it to the letter." Ben shook his hand then told him "I sure hope you have answers for me soon I'm still losing calves and sleep over this mess."

"We'll do the best we can Ben." he told him, "No promises though, these things take time and aren't always so definitive."

Karen told Ben "Until they come back let's put the whole thing out of our minds and relax. We've got enough to do on the farm to keep us busy without worrying for almost a month." But both still waited anxiously every day for the call from the lab wondering if they'd finally get those answers.

When the lab did call them, it was on a Friday, the day Karen was so busy getting ready for the Farmer's Market. The lab tech told Ben he should come over to talk to him personally rather than on the phone because he had several charts and other information to show him. Karen had to stay and finish her baking, so Ben drove over alone. On the way, he was believing they must have found something if they have papers and charts for me to look at and he became hopeful.

The receptionist told the lab tech Ben was there and escorted him into his office. After a short conversation, he said, "Well, let's go over all these tests, Ben." He opened a folder and started reading off the results. "The forage in your pasture is fine. As a matter of fact, there is a nice variety of vegetation that's very nutritional for the cows. Your stored hay is fine too, no molds or bacteria found. The whitewash in the barn is the run of the mill formula, no lead or other additives. The water they are drinking from the pond is fine too. Not any toxic algae blooms there but it did show some disturbing details." The tone of the tech's voice changed to very serious and he cleared his throat. "Ben, I have to tell you, I don't know how it's happening, but you have serious problems."

"What are you talking about?" Ben asked. "Did you find something?" Ben sat forward trying to look at the sheets of paper and charts the technician was holding in his hands.

"The water tests came back with dangerous levels of lead in it." He told him. "Ben, that's not the worst. It also showed traces of Sodium Hydroxide and Dichloromethane in it plus Benzine, Xylene, Tulene, and others. Those are serious toxic chemicals." He said shaking his head.

"What? I had our water tested last year and it was okay." Ben told him.

"Well, I don't know how anybody could have missed these results." The lab tech said. "It's all high levels of pollution. Look, the analysis is right here." He turned the papers around so Ben could see them. Ben scanned the long chemical names plus the percentages that were in his water and then sat back.

"How the hell could any of that be in our water," Ben asked, taking his hat off and running his fingers through his hair. "The cows drink from the pond and the well on the farm has always been good water. You must have messed up the test somehow, those results can't be right."

"That's the reason we took so long to get back to you," the tech said. "We ran the water samples more than once to be sure it was correct. These findings are correct Ben, your water on the farm is seriously compromised, it's not safe. A filter won't even take these things out and the lead along with much of the other compounds accumulates in your body. Dichloromethane turns into hydrochloric acid after a while. There's corrosion inhibitors in your water also including so much more." Then he asked Ben, "Is this the same source for the water you used in your home?"

Ben was quiet for a moment. His eyes opened wide as if he'd seen a ghost and he said. "Yes, it is!" Instantly he became very concerned for Karen, who drank and used the water all the time.

The lab tech kept talking, "These are all also suspected or known carcinogens, they can cause cell mutations along with illnesses. They shouldn't be in contact with your skin or eyes."

Ben thought of Karen again and the awful rash she had for months as well as her forgetfulness. She was seeing a doctor for fertility problems too. He realized there was a connection between each of those problems and was getting even more concerned and upset. He asked. "Tell me, do you think those chemicals in our water could hurt a person if they drank it?"

"Don't drink this water, Ben. We don't exactly know the extent of what all these chemicals mixing together could do. They probably make new compounds, even more toxic."

Ben asked, "How about a cow, it's so much bigger than a person if she was carrying a calf and drank this water, would it cause problems?"

"I believe it could cause all kinds of problems for a growing calf especially, possible birth defects, nerve damage, many things could go wrong. I'm telling you, Ben, there are serious toxic chemicals in your water. You've got to understand this, it's important, it's not fit for man or beast."

Ben felt as if his breath was being sucked out of him. He took the papers the lab tech was handing him. They both stood, Ben took off his cap again and wiped his hand across his forehead. He let out a long breath and said: "Whew, this is not what I had expected or wanted."

"I'm really sorry Ben, so sorry," the lab tech told him feeling the weight himself of the bad news he had to relate. "I know how important good water is, especially on a farm."

On the way back home thoughts and questions were going through his head faster than he could connect with them. He was so worried about Karen's health and state of the whole farm. A car came toward him as he drifted into the opposite lane and the driver blew its horn to get Ben's attention. He corrected his driving just in time. He almost had an accident, he was so preoccupied with the test results.

What happened to his water on the farm? His Dad never had any problems like this in all the years he'd farmed the place. What had changed? Ben was farming the same way his Dad did. The only difference was he had some pieces of more modern equipment and was planting the more modern seed. What is so different now causing such damage? There was news of acid rain in the Northeast from factories and people burning coal. It was making trees die off, but the chemicals in his water were much worse than those issues.

The only thing different in his area was he had a new neighbor, Blair Coleman who'd put in a hunting cabin. *I should check the place out again and be sure to get inside this time,* He thought.

He'd have to tell Karen the bad news, then start buying drinking and house water for them, but what was he going to do regarding the herd? The cows couldn't keep drinking the water either and his milking equipment was cleaned with the same water. This problem was huge and devastating. It got bigger the more he got to thinking. Oh, my God, he thought, I can't farm anymore if this isn't fixed. I'll lose everything, and Karen, what has this done to her already? Why aren't I showing the effects of this like she is? Then he thought about how she usually hand-washes the dishes and she enjoys taking long baths, while he takes a quick shower. She drinks lots of homemade lemonade but he's drinking Monster energy drinks all the time. She holds onto the hose and is getting the mist from it when she waters the garden he thought. He realized she's had a lot more exposure than I have.

Why didn't this show up when it was tested last year at the college he wondered? By the time he pulled into his driveway, he was fuming, and his concerns were multiplying. Karen had been watching for him and greeted him at the door. He gave her a long tender kiss and held her tightly.

She looked at him funny and said "Wow, you missed me a lot, didn't you? How did it go at the lab?" she asked. "Did they find anything this time?"

He held her by both arms while looking deep into her eyes. "Karen, I don't even know how to tell you this, our water all over the farm is toxic. It's got such bad chemicals in it."

"Don't be silly Ben, our water is fine." She turned, went to the sink, and filled a glass with water. "Look, it's cold, clear and tastes good." She raised the glass to take a sip.

Ben stopped her saying "No, you can't drink that Karen, I'll buy us good water. Come here and look at these papers from EnBioApp." He showed her the pages of charts and graphs plus the technical information the lab had detailed for them. They both studied the papers with the unfamiliar names of the chemicals. They leaned back in their chairs and stared sadly at the pile of information, realizing this was a major blow to their dreams plus it could also mean financial ruin.

Karen asked, "Ben . . . how, why?"

"I don't know Karen, but I sure as hell am going to find out." He was so angry now and determined to get to the bottom of the pollution. Ben's eyes caught the picture of Kasey getting his award at the college again. He'd start there, he thought, I'll ask Professor Herrick why this problem didn't show up in the first tests done by the Science Department they did for him a year ago at the Valley View campus last year.

Chapter Seven

THE SECRETARY showed Ben into Professor Herrick's office and said he'd be right with him. He was finishing up lecturing to a class. Ben leaned back in the expensive maroon leather chair and looked around at the certificates, awards, and photos Herrick had on his walls. The office had the look of an important along with well-paid professional and Ben was beginning to wonder to himself why he was questioning this man's test results. Professor Herrick soon entered, gave Ben a handshake, then took a seat behind his big cluttered desk. They chatted a little regarding the awards ceremony and Junior Science Camp his nephew Kasey had attended.

Herrick leaned forward and remarked, "I remember him, he had quite a handshake for a young guy. His project was great, he'll make a good scientist someday."

Ben answered, "Well, I think he wants to be a farmer the same as his Dad."

"Oh," Herrick replied in a flat tone, looking down at his desktop, "Well that would be nice." But Ben could tell he didn't consider that a good career choice. Then Herrick asked, "How can I help you, Ben?" Ben told him he ran tests again, but this time took them to EnBioApp in Mansfield.

"You shouldn't have done that," Herrick said. "I gave you the test results already."

"Well, I still am losing calves and wanted to know why," Ben replied. He pulled out all the papers he had gotten from EnBioApp in Mansfield then passed them over to the professor who started scanning them briefly.

Ben waited a moment then asked, "Did you read the results for the tests on our water at the farm?"

"Uh, let's see what exactly it shows here." Herrick adjusted his glasses and was studying the papers along with the charts without saying anything except "Oh," and then he was silent.

Ben spoke up, "Can you tell me why all those chemicals showed up in my water when they ran the tests at EnBioApp, and it didn't show up when you did them for us a year ago?"

Professor Herrick looked at the papers quickly again then said "Humph . . . surprising. This pollution had to happen *after* we ran the tests."

"No, I don't think so," Ben said firmly, "the water must have been toxic when you did the first tests, my calves were dying then, it's why Doc Morris brought those samples to you. Why didn't you tell me our water was so bad? My wife and I have been drinking it for quite a while now. My herd drinks it too. I should have been told it was toxic." Professor Herrick's chair made a groaning sound as he turned around, then pulled out a file cabinet drawer. He got out a thin folder with Ben's name on it, flipped it open and started reading.

"Well, let's find out what we did for you." He was impatiently turning what few pages were in the folder. "I see we checked for algae, coliform and E. coli bacteria. We also checked for herbicides in the water and pond on your property. We checked the turbidity, he lowered his glasses looking at Ben and said in case you don't know that's suspended earth sediments, no problems there. Nothing came up with any measurable results that could cause problems." he said in a flat matter of fact voice.

"You never checked for any heavy metals or toxic chemicals? You only did those tests?" Ben asked astounded.

"Now, why should we check for chemicals like that on your farm when you live way out there in the boonies far away from town Ben? Where on earth could it have come from?" he leaned back in his chair, folded his arms across his chest and gave Ben an annoyed look.

"I'd have thought if you were doing a thorough testing job you would have looked for anything and everything," Ben answered firmly.

Herrick was annoyed. "Look, Ben, all that takes too much time and its expensive. We had no reason to suspect any chemical contamination except what might normally be found on your small farm. Besides, we were doing you a favor and saved you money. I know you dairy farmers are having a hard time making a living. I thought you'd be more grateful," he said impatiently. Professor Herrick was trying to end the conversation. "Now, is there anything else you want? I have another class to attend to."

Ben sat silent for a moment taking the Professor's comments in. This guy actually thought he had been helping him by not doing all the proper tests. Ben looked at the wall behind Professor Herrick's desk and noticed a picture of Herrick and Blair Coleman posing with golf clubs.

"I see you know my neighbor Blair Coleman," he said pointing to the photo and realizing they were friends.

"Oh, yes we golf together; great guy, great guy. He does a lot for our Science Program here. Well, your nephew benefitted from his generosity with Junior Science Camp, Coleman helps cover the costs for it."

Ben thought this guy's dismissing this, and smiling and acting as if nothing's wrong, he doesn't realize how bad this is for us. He's trying to cover his ass for doing a sloppy job. Ben pointed to the EnBioApp lab results again and pressed him with more questions. "Tell me what you think could cause these types of chemicals to get into my water?"

Professor Herrick rocked back and forth in his leather chair and said flatly "I have absolutely no idea Ben, no idea at all, I'm not a detective you know. I'm sorry, I must leave for a class. Again, I'm sorry you're having problems, but I can't help you anymore, please let yourself out." He quickly shook Ben's hand without looking him in the eyes and left the room, loudly pulling the door shut behind him. Ben heard him mutter "ungrateful, waste of my time!" before it shut all the way.

Ben sat for a moment contemplating the brush off he had just gotten. I certainly didn't get any answers or apologies from him, he thought, he gave me a bunch of excuses plus he thought he had done nothing wrong. He even acted as if I should thank him for saving me money on the tests he didn't do right. "What an incompetent ass you are!" Ben said to Herrick's empty chair. Ben left the room and walked down the hallway towards the exit and noticed another picture on the wall just outside Herrick's office. This one was a framed newspaper clipping from the Tioga Gazette of Professor Herrick holding an oversized check for $50,000. The caption read *MetInverse Enterprises, donates large sum to Professor's research project.* Blair Coleman was standing there with Herrick holding the check.

Ben called Warren on his cell phone when he got back into his truck and told him everything that had happened when he went to the Science Department. He told him there were tests he never ran, what Professor Herrick had said, plus the photos he had seen.

"Warren, I know now the cows are getting poisoned and it's why the calves are dying, but even worse, Karen's gotten sick from it too. This is terrible, can you help me get to the bottom of this mess?"

Warren told him "Ben, you're family, I'll do anything I can to help you and Karen out. Give me a call when you want me to do something, anything, and hang in there buddy."

Later, Ben told Karen all about his discussion with Professor Herrick in addition to how quickly he had changed the subject when he tried to pin him down concerning not doing tests he should have plus his superior attitude. He told her also there were pictures he had seen of Coleman and Herrick together, especially the one in the hallway with Herrick holding the check for $50,000.

"Karen, do you know what MetInverse Enterprises, does? What type of business is it?"

"No, I don't Ben, but have you heard there's this thing called a computer and an Internet?" They even have Google which is something like an encyclopedia with answers to your questions," she told him teasing. Ben hated computers and didn't have much use for them. She had tried in vain to get him comfortable enough to use one for crop and dairy information, but he would click away in all the wrong places and get so hopelessly lost he could never get what he wanted on the screen. She gave up trying to teach him when he got so frustrated, he started swearing at the computer screen. Instead of being enlightened by the internet it put him into a frustrating dark mood.

"I can Google it for you," she said and opened her laptop. "Be sure to remember me on Secretary's Day."

MetInverse Enterprises popped up with a slick professional homepage. The business had several branches and stated they were an *Innovative Force . . . Pioneers in their Field.* It also said they had *State of the Art Production Facilities.*

"There's more than one plant listed," Karen said. "It also lists Blair Coleman as Owner and Chief Operations Manager. This guy really is a big shot."

"Umm Karen, what the heck do they do?" Ben asked impatiently.

"I'm looking, I'm looking . . . Oh, here it is," she read off some details. "Our company strips and resurfaces metal components for industry, so the frameworks and parts can be used again saving the manufacturer thousands of dollars. We are experts in the process of inversing coated, plated or sprayed metal finishes."

Ben was silent for a moment staring at the screen and thinking about what that statement meant. Then he asked "They strip metal? That means they must strip paint or finishes off?"

"Yes, I believe so Ben. There's a whole alphabetical list of things they say they can remove. They take off Baked on Coatings, Chrome and Copper Coatings, Electrostatic Coatings, Epoxy Coatings, Flame Retardant Coatings, Powder Coatings, Zinc Coatings, and more. It says *Ask and our professional scientists will create a program for your material recovery needs."*

Karen had no idea what those coatings were, but she did know what chrome was and asked, "They can take shiny chrome back off the metal, how the heck do they do that?"

"With seriously toxic chemicals Karen," he answered shaking his head, "really bad." Ben felt as if he was sinking into a hole and it was closing over him. He had a good idea now what had gotten into his water, however, he needed to figure out how and why it was happening, and if there was a way to stop it and fix the problem.

Warren and Ben met up a couple of days later at Grandma's Kitchen in Mansfield over eggs, home fries, bacon, and biscuits.

They were talking about what Karen had found on the computer when a tall, muscular man came into the diner then sat at the counter near them. Warren was so involved in shoving food in his mouth while listening to Ben he didn't notice him at first. When he recognized who it was though, he called out to him.

"Hey, Sandy how the hell are you doing?"

Ben recognized Sandy too, and said: "You still making a living poking little holes in the ground?"

Sandy turned around, recognized the guys and said "Well, look at what the cat dragged in here. Sure am, and it's paying damn good too." He told them nodding his head and smiling. Sandy was the local well driller and it was his truck Ben had seen go into the Coleman property when the construction first began up there.

"Come on over and sit with us," he told him. Sandy grabbed his coffee and slid in next to Warren.

"Move over there fatso," he told him. Warren and Sandy had played football together in high school and were old friends.

Warren fired right back at Sandy, "Well, look at the gut on you."

"Me . . . Look at the pot belly you have now, when exactly are you due, must be any day now right? Have you picked a name?" Sandy said right back poking Warren in the ribs. Both men weren't fat, just stocky and muscular, yet they teased each other like that each time they met.

Ben spoke up, "Hey Sandy, you put a well on the Coleman property next to me, how'd it go?"

"It took too long, yes I made lots of money off that one, but the guy was strange. I hit water after two days, told him it was five gallons a minute, plenty of water for a hunting cabin, however, he said: "Keep going, I don't want to call you back to make it deeper if it dries up in a long hot spell." I told him I didn't believe that would happen, but he was determined to make it a lot deeper, so I kept drilling. Soon I hit rock with big layers of quartz in it. It slowed my drill way down.

By the time I drilled through all the quartz rock, I was right at the limit of how deep my rig could go, and it's a big one. I charged Coleman enough to put a good down payment on the new bass boat I wanted after I paid all my expenses. He didn't even blink once when I handed him the bill, my type of customer." Sandy said and slapped the table chuckling. "Now, if I can only find time off work to fish and have fun." The pair both knew how hard it was to find free time and nodded their heads.

Sandy added, "Hey, we should get together on my new boat sometime, go on over to Cowanesque, I hear there's big bass in there."

Warren answered, "Yeah, we should." However, in the men's minds, they doubted how all three of them could find any time soon in their busy schedules to connect and do that.

"So, Sandy," Warren continued, "He had lots of water there and had no reason to have water delivered?"

"Have water brought in there, hell no, he had plenty. That well ended up tapping into a big aquifer for your whole area. He'd never have to bring water in no matter how bad the drought, all he had to do was hook up a strong pump, and he was good to go. He didn't want me to install the pump though. Said he had a friend in the business and was going to use him. Hell, I could have charged him even more."

Ben and Warren listened intently to his words while remembering the Water truck they'd seen pumping water into Coleman's well. Sandy was saying something completely different from what was happening at the well. The men tipped the waitress, they said goodbye to Sandy who left after they promised to get together for a fishing trip.

Still at the table, Ben lowered his voice and said: "Warren, you don't want to hear this, but I need to get inside his cabin."

Warren looked around at the other diners to see if anyone was listening to them then he leaned back in towards Ben, lowered his voice too and asked. "Go back up there again Ben? Are you sure? We didn't see anything the last time. Remember what Karen said about the game cameras recording us? How do we know we won't be filmed and charged with trespassing or breaking and entering? Ben, we could both go to jail over this."

"Yes, I know its private property, but something suspicious is happening. I don't see Coleman going in there with any buddies to hunt and I don't hear any rifles shooting either. There are no four wheelers running around. You know how sounds travel up on my hill. I'd hear the noise of their engines if they were. If his cabin was supposed to be for him and his buddies, why isn't he using it? That's an important question Warren. Remember when we looked through the window and saw the table with the papers on it? I want to see what those are, you going to go with me or am I going by myself?"

Warren thought for a moment and answered, "I'm in, call when you're ready to do it."

"How about next Wednesday?" Ben asked. "We'd have less chance of getting caught in the middle of the week."

"Okay, I'll be out to your place next Wednesday Ben, now we better go get our work done today before its time to eat another meal."

Chapter Eight

KAREN WAS worried about both of them trespassing again on the Coleman property. She warned them to look carefully for game cams and get out of there if they spotted any. "What if someone shows up and catches you?" She asked.

"They won't catch us, Karen, we'll be careful."

They hiked up through his property as before then came out in the woods near the cabin and seeing no cars or trucks were around the cabin, they moved a little closer.

"If you were Coleman where would you put game cams?" Warren asked Ben.

"Probably on the trees by the porch so he could see the front door, look around at those trees over there," Ben said pointing to a group of maples. They both carefully looked for the small camouflaged square boxes and didn't find any. Believing it was safe, they walked up to the porch. Again, the door was locked when Warren tried it. Still rattling the doorknob, he asked: "How the hell are we going to get in there?"

"I don't know," Ben answered. "I want to see those papers Warren. We've got to find a way." The windows on the porch were locked too. They walked around the outside looking for a way to enter. The back door was locked up. Then Warren found a window up high on the side that he could push open and they thought one of them could go through it. Warren said I'll try it while you watch to see if anyone comes up the dirt road. He had trouble however getting through it and Ben had to help by pushing him on his backside. It was a tight fit for Warren and they both got laughing picturing him getting stuck in the window frame. "You've been eating way too many of those Bavarian cream donuts Warren. I'm going to leave you here if you can't get your fat ass through this window," he told him, then chuckled at the thought of Warren wedged into the window with his feet stuck out on one side and his head stuck into the room.

When Warren finally got inside there was a loud thump as he hit the floor and Ben told him, "Don't break anything in there Warren, I know how clumsy you are. Now, will ya go unlock the damn door for me so I can come in too?"

Warren was looking around and said "Man, this is so sparse for a hunting cabin. There isn't much of anything here, only water jugs piled at the sink. Why isn't he using the new well he had drilled?"

Ben came inside as soon as Warren opened the door and told him. "He did put in a new well, I heard them drilling it every day and remember Sandy told us he struck good water?" Ben said, "He's got a kitchen area, look there may be a bedroom back there and a bathroom over there."

"Good, I have to go," Warren said.

"No, you can't go stupid, they might be able to tell we were here," Ben said.

Warren stepped into the small bathroom to check it out anyway. "That's funny", he shouted back, "there's no water in here either when I turn on the faucet. And, he's got one of those electric toilets, you know the kind that cooks the crap and later you pull out a drawer and dump the ashes. I always wondered if they stink when they're cooked?" He pulled out the drawer and took a sniff.

Ben yelled back. "It's not funny there's no water Warren, there must be a reason for it. Warren stop sniffing the crappy ashes and come here. Look at these maps and entries into this log." he pushed the papers towards Warren. "And here's a chart showing the geology and layers of rock and soil on this hill. Remember the science project Kasey did? This looks similar to the diagrams he made."

Warren looked at what he was pointing to. "There's gaps and pockets in there see they're circled for a reason. And, look someone's marked right where the well has been drilled. That thing is deep, over 200 feet. He must have hit water going down so far. He had to hit big pockets of water, Sandy said he thought they were into the whole aquifer for our area."

Ben started reading the handwritten log off to Warren. "Water delivery, July 7th, 3,750 gallons . . . August 10th, Water delivery, 3,000 gallons, all these entries have the initials KS after them and there are several pages the same with his initials including gallon amounts."

Warren looked at Ben and said, "All that water being delivered to his well and there's no water in this cabin? This isn't right, could it be his well won't hold enough water and is leaking it all out somewhere through a big crack in the rock down under the ground or something? Or could it be his pump isn't strong enough to pull water up from such a depth?"

"Warren, do you have your fancy cell phone with you?"

"Yeah, but Ben remember, you live in the boonies, there isn't any signal here."

"I know, I know, doesn't it take pictures without a signal though?" Ben asked pointing to the log and charts.

"Sure does" and Warren took out his phone and started snapping pictures of the charts.

"Take pictures of the water jugs and this whole room too. I want all the pictures you can get." Warren swung his phone around and clicked away even going into the bathroom for more pictures including the drawer of ashes from the toilet.

"Maybe this is his idea of roughing it," Ben said shrugging his shoulders. "With all the money he's supposed to have, he could have built an awesome man toy place for him and his buddies."

They got joking about their own ideas for a man cave again and the plans got bigger and bigger. Warren decided he wanted a dune buggy rather than a four-wheeler to run the trails, and he'd have a lake put in not just a pond, and stock it with bass so he could fish from the new fancy bass boat with the sparkly paint job he'd have too. Oh, and a hot babe to take the fish he caught off the hook for him.

"Hey," Ben said, "I know your wife, she wouldn't like that."

Warren replied, "The hot babe is Amy, my wife, she's smokin'!"

Ben told him, "Stop already, spare me the details, you're talking about my big sister!"

For Ben's mancave he wanted one of those huge stainless-steel barbeque/smoker combinations and a freezer full of steaks and racks of ribs to cook anytime he wished. Warren added the idea of speakers in every corner of their fantasy man cave so they could have surround sound while watching the sports and movies in the home theatre they'd install. The fantasies got more and more elaborate.

"You know what else I want?" Ben asked. "I want to talk to that Water truck driver. I've noticed him around town before. You can't miss his beat up old green truck with the rust on the sides of the tank. Let's check out this MetInverse Enterprises too. Now, we've got to be careful and leave this place exactly as we found it and get out of here." They put everything back where it was, went out the door and locked it behind them before heading to the farmhouse.

Karen looked forward to every Saturday now because she had loyal customers returning every week to make purchases plus Melvin visited her booth. She was earning enough to start putting some savings away. She had made good friends at the Farmer's Market. They all joked with each other as they set up their booths to get ready for the shoppers. Often someone was struggling with their canopy trying to open it by themselves and a vendor stopped what they were doing to lend them a hand. Cindy, a vendor near Karen's spot was struggling with the legs of her canopy and Karen went over to help her get them extended properly.

“Looks as if you need extra hands here Cindy,” Karen said helping her steady the frame of the canopy.

“Oh, thank you, Karen. It’s like I’m wrestling with an octopus this morning!” Cindy told her as she pulled on a tall metal leg. Together they managed to extend the four metal legs to the same height and get them locked in place.

“You’re a lifesaver, Karen,” Cindy told her. “Now, I’ve got to get my stuff set out. How are you doing this morning?”

“I’m almost ready now.” Karen said, then noticing the space beside Cindy was unusually empty she asked, “Where’s your neighbor this morning, sleeping in?”

Cindy’s face got serious and sad as she said “I guess you haven’t heard. Her father committed suicide last week. “I feel so sorry for her.”

“What? Oh my God, what happened to make him want to do something so drastic?” Karen asked.

“Well, he was a widower and his kids had all grown and left home. None of them wanted to stay in farming. My neighbor next door here sold homemade soaps. The rest of his family were more interested in tech jobs or something they didn’t have to work long hours at like the farm. Her father was still trying to keep the farm going. It’d been in his family for four generations and he expected to hand it on down to another family farmer. But he got arthritis quite bad and couldn’t take care of planting and harvesting the crops anymore. It takes physical strength to hook up the farm equipment. He had a series of other setbacks on top of his health issues and they thought he gave up because he got so discouraged. They found him by a big tree out by his farm pond. It looked as if he just got off his tractor and shot himself. My heart goes out to her."

"That's terrible, I feel sorry for his family. I can't imagine ever getting so discouraged I would do that." Karen said saddened by the news.

Cindy answered "I read an article about the high rates of suicide among farmers. Old farmers like him were born on the farm. Most of them started driving a tractor at 10 years of age or sooner if they could reach the brake pedal. They never got pushed to learn anything else in school because they were from farming families and only expected to be a farmer too. Most of these farmers have worked seven days a week since they were a child doing chores. They don't know how to go through a day not working and are lost. Farming is their pride and self-worth. Their life is so woven into the animals, the soil, crops and the farm that losing it to them is losing their own identity. There's no reason to go to the feed store with no stock or to buy seed for planting anymore when the farm fails, and animals are sold off. They don't see their friends at machinery auctions or farm coop meetings. The regular milk truck with the driver they've known for years doesn't even show up to collect their milk anymore. They lose all their normal social connections.

Farmers work independently and enjoy being their own boss and never unload their personal struggles to anyone. They only talk of crop failures or machinery breakdowns but not their own emotional breakdowns. They've been taught to "tough it out" so they don't ask for help. A failing farm and perhaps even losing the farm that's been in the family for generations is too much for them and they see suicide as the only way out in a moment of desperation. It's happening more and more these days and it is really so sad."

"That's tragic news but thank you for explaining it, Cindy. I understand it better now. I'm going to be sure it never happens to Ben. We should get a sympathy card and have everyone sign it for your neighbor here." Karen said.

A customer over at Karen's booth was holding up a loaf of bread and called out "Hey Karen, are you open for business yet?"

"Yes, I'll be right there." She answered and said goodbye to Amy. Karen waited on her customer and then noticed Melvin coming her way.

"What can I get you today Sweetie?" she asked Melvin as he approached her table. His smile faded as soon as she asked him that. He straightened up and looked sternly at her.

Very firmly but in a quiet way, he said "Karen, you know I like you, but please don't call me Sweetie, Honey, Dearie or any of the crap. Why is it when a person gets older people start addressing them like a little child? It's called Senior Speak like you can't talk to us normal because we don't have a brain anymore." Speaking more gently he said. "My name is Melvin, okay?"

"Okay, Melvin." She replied, slightly embarrassed. Karen thought about what Melvin had said. He seemed a little cranky today, but as soon as he had given her that speech his mood changed, and he became as cheerful as usual.

"What ya got for cookies this week?" he asked.

Karen showed him her big almond and chocolate chip cookies. She had figured out how to make them, so they were crispy on the edges and soft in the middle and they tasted delicious. She gave Melvin a sample. He usually got samples from almost everyone selling any food at the market such as small cubes of smoked gouda cheese from the Amish lady, some cherries or fruit of the week from another. He'd also taste a couple of grape tomatoes or a slice of melon from a produce vendor. He'd even have crackers and dip with a sip of Kraft beer. She wondered sometimes if he wasn't snacking through the market for a quick meal. No one minded though. He was a fixture at the market, and everyone enjoyed seeing him each week. If he didn't show up, they'd get worried. Karen handed him the bag of country bread and chocolate chip cookies he had chosen.

The old man pulled the loaf of bread back out of the package, held it to his nose and took a long sniff.

"My wife Grace used to make bread like this for us every week. This reminds me of her, she's been gone for eight years now. Nothing is the same on our farm anymore. I'm on my own, even the stock is gone." Melvin said sadly.

"I didn't know you were a farmer. My husband Ben and I have a small dairy. It's called Hilltop Farm and sits overlooking Sugar Creek." She told him.

"What's your last name, Karen?" Melvin asked curiously.

"It's Carlisle, Karen Carlisle, my husband is Ben."

"Heck, I was friends with your father-in-law. We even sold heifers and steers to each other. He was a good farmer and friend." Melvin told her. "I didn't see him often because we lived so far apart, but we'd run into each other at machinery auctions and at the feed mill sometimes."

Karen thought Ben would enjoy talking to Melvin about his Dad, so she asked him. "Melvin we'd like you to come to dinner at our place some night."

"I'd love to. Anybody who bakes bread as good as this must be a good cook too." Melvin said munching on his cookie. "Besides, I get awful lonely eating supper all by myself."

They exchanged phone numbers and Karen promised to call him soon and set up a date for the meal. Melvin said goodbye and Karen turned to wait on another customer.

Chapter Nine

A FEW DAYS later Ben and Warren headed over to the MetInverse Enterprises plant to see what they could find out.

The low, one story red brick building for the company had a generic white sign out front with the words MetInverse Enterprises spelled out in plain black lettering. There was a large parking lot on the left side with a scattering of cars and pickups. One of the cars stood out as it was an expensive, new yellow Corvette.

"Someone's making money here," Warren said. There was another lot out back of the plant and they noticed various empty shells of copiers and other machinery in clusters around the edges of the lot. Many had labels for IBM and Xerox on them.

"Wow, both of them are important companies, he must have big contracts," Ben said.

There were only a few small windows in the building, low shrubs around its base, and a single front door of glass and aluminum with a sign stating it was the office.

Big air conditioners and fans dotted the surface of the flat roof.

Ben said, “Warren, come up with a reason to go into the building so we can find out what’s going on in there.” Warren answered “Me, why do I have to do it, why not you?”

“Because Coleman might be in there and he could remember me from the auction when he was bidding on the land he got. He doesn’t know you, come on think of something.”

Warren looked away for a minute and then said: “Well, I could say I’m collecting donations for Little League, Kasey plays on a team and they always need money for uniforms, travel, and equipment.”

“Great idea, go do it,” Ben said pushing on him to get him out the truck’s door.

“Okay, okay, I’m going. Don’t be so pushy.” Warren got out of the truck and walked over to the building and disappeared through the front door. Ben sat there wishing he could be in there too. Then he heard a truck coming and was surprised when he turned and looked. It was the familiar old beat up green truck with the word Water spelled out on its side. It traveled around to the back of the building. Ben jumped out of his pickup and walked to a spot where he could watch what was going on without anyone seeing him. The tanker backed in next to another truck with a red cab. It was the same size as the Water truck and made to hold liquids similar to his. Ben watched as the Water truck driver unhooked a hose from the red truck and went up a ladder and put it into the top of his Water truck. He pulled up on a lever and started pumping the contents of the red truck into his.

It took a few minutes and soon the driver replaced the hose, jumped in the cab of his Water truck and pulled away. When he left, Ben could see Hazmat signs on the back of the red truck parked there warning it was a toxic chemical carrier. He left where he had been on a run to his pickup. Warren was sitting there waiting when he jumped in.

"Where in the hell have you been?" Warren asked, annoyed.

"Never mind that right now Warren, we've got to follow this truck," Ben told him.

Warren asked "What . . . that old Water truck?"

Ben was looking at the intersection of the main road and the plant's driveway. "Yes, which way did it turn, did you notice, left or right?" He scanned down the road both ways and spotted the hulk of the truck off in the distance and quickly pulled out to go the same way. They kept the truck in their vision, but they stayed far enough back so as not to cause suspicion by the driver if he looked behind him.

"What happened in the office Warren, did you find out anything?" Ben asked, keeping his eyes on the truck they were following while steering.

"I couldn't get past the reception area to see anything. I did get a $50 donation for the team though." and he waved the cash.

"Too bad it's probably dirty money," Ben said.

It wasn't long before they were on Route 529 and traveling out of town on the narrow winding country roads. Ben told Warren what he had seen behind the building by the loading docks and the Hazmat signs on the red truck parked there.

"So, you believe this guy, Keith Tynor is hauling chemicals he pumped from that truck, Ben?"

"Yes, I do Warren. Let's see what he does now."

The roads were narrowing down more as they passed farm after farm where cows were grazing in pastures and farmers were tending crops. The farms had neatly painted houses and barns and were well kept with corn tall in the fields. Other farms had skeletons of barns with boards missing, the roof caving in and fields neglected and overgrown because the owner had abandoned farming or farming had abandoned him.

Warren said, "Boy, I bet these kids living out here have a long ride on the school bus."

They traveled through Roseville, a town not more than two roads crossing each other and a church and went further out into the country. Finally, the Water truck turned off onto a dirt road. Ben let him get way ahead of his pickup, the Water truck was sending up a dust cloud behind it which was helping Ben's vehicle not to be seen following him. He was further back on a dirt road that wound through a forest area with only an occasional hunting camp tucked back in the trees here and there. They could tell the Water truck turned off onto a narrow logging road marked *PRIVATE PROPERTY – Logging Operation – KEEP OUT.* Ben pulled his pickup over in a wide spot in the road and they watched the truck go on up the logging road and out of sight. He and Warren sat there talking about the Water truck and the chemical truck they saw at MetInverse and both speculated he was probably dumping what may be his toxic load back in those woods.

"Warren, I'm going to find out for sure what's going on and he's the one to tell me." He started his pickup back up, drove forward and pulled it across the entrance to the logging road. When the Water truck came back down the logging road and noticed the pickup blocking him, he quickly braked and honked his horn. When the guys didn't move, he shut his motor off and got out of his cab.

"Hey fellas," the driver walked closer and said, "I've got to get out of here, you have to move your pickup out of the way, what are you, hunters?"

Warren told him "Yeah, we're hunters alright, looking for answers today, you got any?" and he got out and started walking towards the driver.

Ben stopped him saying "I'll handle this Warren." He turned to the driver and said, "Just what were you doing back in there?"

The driver hesitated, he was looking at the toe of his shoe as it drew a line in the dirt, then he said "I'm hauling water back into the logging camp. They need it for equipment radiators and stuff."

"You didn't have water in your truck, I know what you were carrying, I saw you loading it at MetInverse Enterprises," Ben told him.

The driver straightened up and looked suddenly quite worried. "Who are you guys and what business is it of yours anyways?"

Ben told him "You hauled water next to my property too, and now I've got serious problems on my farm. You're dumping chemicals for MetInverse Enterprises, aren't you?"

The driver rubbed his forehead with his hand and looked down at his feet again shaking his head. He let out a big sigh and his shoulders slumped down. "Look, mister, I'm just doing a job I get paid for. I'm not a young man anymore, there's not much work for a man 69 years old. I gotta sick wife and no damn insurance. I worked hard all my life, only not smart enough. This is the only work I could find so I can pay her medical bills."

Warren told him angrily "But, you're dumping chemicals and polluting the water wherever you do that."

The driver had a guilty look on his face. "All the places I dump are way, way out in the country just like here in these woods. It doesn't hurt anyone."

"Yes, it does!" Ben said loudly. "My wife is sick, and I've lost too many calves. We have no drinking water in our house now and our water has been poisoning the rest of my herd."

The old driver's face got sad and he looked defeated. He apologized saying, "God, I'm sorry, so sorry, I didn't know about that, I never meant to hurt anyone, just doing the job I was paid to do." The pair were trying to understand the man's motives and position. He was the family provider with financial burdens and had to take care of his ill wife.

"Who's paying you to do this?" Ben asked.

"Mr. Coleman, the owner of MetInverse Enterprises. My wife used to work there before she got real sick. She washed small parts off after they came out of the paint strippers. Her clothes always smelled of those chemicals. She said the mist from the vats was so heavy at times it felt as if dew was falling on her. One time she had a hole in her rubber glove when she was unloading parts and didn't know it. When she took it off at the end of the day a whole bunch of her skin came right off too.

She knew then she was messing with bad stuff. I told her to look for another job, anything was better than there, but she didn't want to lose what she had paid in for her benefits, and who would want to hire someone who's sickly on most days?

"It's hard for an older person to find work around here you know. Before she could find another job, she got real sick. She had trouble breathing and everything. Turned out though when she tried to get insurance to pay for the medical bills Coleman said she had something called a pre-existing condition and it wasn't covered. She'd been paying into his insurance program for a long time, however, he said what he had for his employees wouldn't cover her illnesses. We had so many bills from doctor visits, and lab work, and different tests and lots of medicine. She had to get a breathing machine for treatments every day that we had to pay rent on, and medicine to go in it too. You wouldn't believe how much a simple blood test costs, he said disgusted. Nothing was helping and the bills kept coming and coming. Mr. Coleman was real nice and offered me this job to help pay those bills. He pays me in cash, under the table stuff so I don't have to report it. It helps me get her the treatments and medicine she has to have." Keith said, "And it won't mess up my social security either."

Warren asked, "What exactly are you supposed to do for him?"

"At first I was only dumping a few barrels for him. He told me to drive a pickup he had on the back roads and unplug the hole in the barrels and let the liquid run out as I drove along the country roads. One time I got stopped behind a school bus that was letting kids off with those barrels leaking those fluids. When I saw the little kids getting off the bus, I felt real bad. I told him I couldn't do that anymore, so he came up with a new plan. He wanted me to take the chemicals out of town, way out of sight, dump them on the ground where there was a depression in the earth and burn them. I found a place back in the forest where there was an abandoned quarry, drained a pool from my tank out there, but it made such a big, hot fire when I lit it, my eyebrows and hair got scorched. I thought the fire company was going to show up it was so big, or I'd set fire to the woods, so I wasn't going burn the stuff either. My face looked like a damn sunburn for over a week."

"Now I show up every few weeks and pump out the trucks which are parked behind the buildings into mine. I take the liquids to different places in the country and pump it into the wells he has."

Ben asked, "You mean you take chemicals from more than one of his plants?"

"Yes, I do all three, Waverly and Elmira in New York and Mansfield in PA."

"What about the trucks that are parked behind his plant, why don't they haul the liquids away to a toxic waste facility?"

"Coleman said it was too expensive. Those trucks are just for holding the liquids and for show when the Inspectors come around. They pull them out and move them back in once and a while to make it look as if they've gone somewhere, but they never actually leave the lot."

Warren spoke up "Wait a minute, I've seen you pumping water into the kid's pool at the Recreation

Park. Are you using the same truck to haul water for swimming that had those chemicals in it?"

"I rinses my tank out real good before I fill any pools," Keith said defensively.

Ben asked wondering "And how do you rinse it?"

"I have a place where I can pull my truck down to the water at Sugar Creek and I do it there. I pump creek water in and pump it back out until it's clear and I don't see any more of that rainbow looking stuff on the water." Keith answered.

"Incredible!" Ben said, "This just keeps getting worse and worse. You're putting toxic chemicals into the stream too. You know this has to stop don't you, you can't keep doing this."

"I'm going to lose my job, aren't I?" he said worriedly.

Ben answered "I'm sorry but this whole thing is wrong, it's wrong, and you know it, don't you? Promise me you'll stop doing this." Ben said to the driver.

"I will, I've been feelin' bad about this for some time. I'll stop. Coleman never even reported most of the bad chemicals he uses at his plant to the government. He said, "What they don't know can't hurt me." The old man told them sadly and then turned and walked slowly back to the Water truck. Ben got back into his pickup. Warren hesitated for a minute looking at the old driver before he too turned away and joined Ben. They rode in silence for a while, deep in thought.

Warren asked quietly, "Ben, what are you going to do now?"

"I'm going to meet with Coleman and tell him I'm notifying everyone I know in town their outstanding businessman is really a scumbag poisoning our environment. Did you know I searched through the list of businesses in Pennsylvania that dealt with toxic chemicals and MetInverse wasn't even on the list to be monitored? I'll bet the government doesn't even know what he's been using and disposing of there just as the driver said. There's probably not even enough inspectors to go around. Makes you wonder what other businesses are doing the same thing and getting away with it doesn't it?"

"My mother used to have a saying similar to what the driver said, *what you don't know can't hurt you,*" Warren said.

"Well, that's not true with toxic chemicals in our water is it?" Ben answered.

He was quiet for a few moments and when he spoke up again, he said: "Warren, I have an idea, how would you like to be the owner of a new company?"

"What do you mean?"

Ben said "I want you to confront Coleman face to face and record the conversation, however, I don't know which plant he's at. How about you pretend you have a business needing his services and set up a meeting at his location? Could you do that Warren?"

"I'd be glad to Ben, I'll set something up so I can be in on the fun of nailing this guy."

Ben dropped Warren back off at his car, they said goodbye, and they planned to meet up with each other soon to give Blair Coleman a visit.

Chapter Ten

LATER IN the afternoon, Karen was making a special meal for Melvin's visit. He was such a sweet old gentleman. They chatted every week at the Farmer's Market and she wanted to know him better. She also looked forward to having Ben talk to him about knowing his Dad. She was putting whipped peanut butter frosting on a chocolate layer cake when Melvin's car pulled in the drive. He got out, came up on the porch and knocked on her screen door. She opened it to him standing there looking shy.

"Melvin, I'm so glad you came. Ben is still down in the barn. He's probably almost done with the milking. Why don't you go tell him I said suppers almost ready?" Karen asked.

"Sure," Melvin said. "I can do that." Melvin put his hat back on and headed toward the lights coming out the barn doors. He stepped inside the dairy just as Ben was putting the milker on the last cow he had to do. Melvin heard the familiar "chew-chew-chew-chew" sound of the vacuum pump going. Ben saw him standing there and called out to him.

"Melvin, welcome to our farm, Karen's told me a lot about you." Ben stepped over to him, they shook hands and then stood in the doorway while they talked. "You know a long time ago when I was little I remember my Dad taking me to your farm Melvin. You have a lot more acres over there. I remember a nice place with woods and a fishing pond. He took me back in there a couple of times to fish too but not often. He was always so busy here on this farm." He told him.

Melvin was busy looking around the barn remembering times a few years ago when he had milked in the evenings before supper. There was a heavy metal lid off a milk can sitting upside down on the floor and a mother barn cat and kittens were drinking milk out of it. He looked at the double row of cows eating their evening hay, content now since being milked. They were swinging their tails, and their jaws moved back and forth as they were chewing their hay. He could smell the hay and the nose tingling smell of the manure in the drops. A few white moths were swirling around the bare lightbulbs hanging from the ceiling and barn swallows were flying in and out the open door.

"This barn brings back happy memories." He said to Ben. "Those were good days for my wife and me when we were running our dairy. We raised a daughter on our farm."

"Karen had told me you had been a farmer but aren't doing it anymore. When she told me your last name, I remembered seeing you and your place so long ago." Ben told him. "But, you're not in the dairy business anymore Melvin?"

"No, I got out of it after my wife passed. My daughter got married and left, so I didn't see any reason to keep the dairy going. Besides, I'm too old now to do all the work."

The cow with the milker on mooed and stomped her back foot and Ben said, "She's done, I better take the milker off." He unhooked her and turned off the pump. The milk was sent through plastic tubing right to the refrigeration tank where it was stirred and kept cold until the big milk truck came to get it. Then it was hauled to the processing plant to be turned into drinking milk, cheese, yogurt, ice cream, and other dairy products. Even the whey from the cheesemaking was used as feed for other animals or more food products. Elmer's glue was even a byproduct of milk at one time.

Once Ben had put the milking equipment away, he turned off the lights in the barn and milk house while Melvin waited, and then they walked back to the house. Karen heard them come in and reminded Ben to leave his boots on the porch, wash up and change his barn clothes.

"Karen, you know I do the same thing every night, Women!" he said winking at Melvin. Karen asked Melvin if he wanted a cup of coffee or tea in the kitchen while they waited for Ben. They sat at the white enamel table chatting about the weather and their day. Tippy came over to Melvin and put his head on his knee to be petted as he did with Ben. Melvin leaned over and started stroking the dog's head affectionately.

"I'm sorry," Karen said. "He thinks everyone should be petting him. Tippy, leave him alone, go lay down in your bed." She pointed to where she wanted the dog to go and lay on an old cushion next to the wall.

"It's okay Karen. I enjoy dogs. Matter of fact I had a farm dog almost like this one that used to help get the cows back to the barn for milking. Now you can herd the cows with those four-wheelers." He paused and said. "My old dog's gone now too."

Karen spoke up and said "Melvin I'm so sorry you've lost your wife. I can't imagine losing my Ben."

"I didn't lose her Karen. I know right where she is, waiting for me. We're apart for a while and we'll be back together again sometime in the future." Melvin answered.

The love on his face when he spoke of his wife was so touching to Karen she reached out and patted his hand. They both sipped their coffee and were silent for a moment. Ben came into the room all clean and smelling good from his quick shower and a fresh change of clothes.

"How are you two doing?" he asked, "and what's for supper? It smells great in here."

Karen said. "It's a surprise, why don't you and Melvin head into the dining room and I'll bring the food in."

"Wow, we're getting fancy tonight, aren't we? Usually, Karen tosses a couple slices of bread at me and hands me the peanut butter jar." Ben told Melvin.

"Ben, you know that's not true!" Karen scolded him.

"No, it's not Melvin. She takes good care of me and her meals are delicious." Ben showed Melvin to the dining room and they sat down at the table. Karen had already put their table settings out for them. Soon she appeared with loaded plates of hot food. Days earlier she had been thinking about what to serve that Melvin might like. He'd enjoy whatever his wife would have made him she decided and settled on roast chicken with mashed potatoes and gravy, baby green peas, stuffing and baking powder biscuits. It was a simple country meal he'd probably had several times. When she put the food on the table for them to pass around and sat down herself, she could see Melvin's eyes almost tear up.

"I haven't had a meal like this in so long Karen." He told her. "Grace used to make this for us. We had such a good life. Thank you for doing all this work."

They loaded their plates and chatted while they ate about the weather and farming and things Melvin remembered when he had been friends with Ben's dad years earlier. Melvin talked to them too regarding how different farming was done now and asked Ben about the new kinds of equipment being used. Then he said "When we had chicken for supper, I used to have to kill one of our flock. I had to catch a fat one, usually, one Grace said wasn't laying good anymore. I'd quickly chop its head off with an ax. Crazy thing would run around for a short time then drop over on its side. I'd have to hold it up by its feet while I plucked the big feathers out. Once you got them gone then you dunked it in hot water to loosen the rest of the feathers and pull them off the carcass. I'd have feathers stuck all over me. Next, I'd singe the fine hair off by holding it close to the flame. After that, I'd take it up to Grace in the kitchen and she'd finish cleaning it and roast it." Melvin told them.

"Wow, so much work just for a meal of chicken Melvin. I traded for this chicken ready to cook at the Farmer's Market. It's a free-range chicken." Karen said.

Melvin laughed and added, "When we were growing up everything we ate, was healthy free-range food, not something from the supermarket. Chicken there comes from big chicken factories where they never get outdoors or see sunlight. Those chickens are kept crowded inside under electric lights all jammed together. They get so sick they put antibiotics in their feed. I read they've done genetic breeding on those birds and their breast meat gets so big they can't walk without falling over frontwards. They're ruining the animals and our food with that factory farming. We never knew how good we had it years ago. Free range," he said chuckling more at those two words. "We had free range everything back then, even the kids were free range."

Ben asked, "Are you doing any farming at all now Melvin? Did you keep chickens or any stock?"

"No, I couldn't take care of stock by myself anymore. I hate seeing the barn empty and not having any animals around though. Besides it's only me now, I don't eat much. I got a jar of peanut butter and bread too." He said laughing. "And I eat those frozen dinners, that's why a real home cooked meal like this is such a special treat," Melvin told them.

"Melvin, you know those frozen dinners aren't good for you the same as the factory chickens, don't you? They're full of sodium and bad for your blood pressure and heart." She told him concerned.

"I don't worry about that stuff anymore Karen. I'll be gone soon anyways," Melvin replied.

"Oh, don't say that Melvin, I enjoy talking to you," Karen told him.

They were finishing up and Melvin asked "Karen, do you mind if I take a couple of those biscuits home? They're so good. You are such a good cook and baker. Ben, you got a treasure here."

Karen said "Sure you can Melvin. I'm going to put leftovers in containers for you too. Ben and I don't need this much food. You sit right there and talk to Ben while I clear things away."

"No, it isn't right for you to do all this cooking and have to clean up too Karen," Ben said as he rose from his chair and grabbed plates. "You stay here with Melvin and I'll clear the table. I know how to stack dishes and put things away. Besides if I don't do my chores Momma Karen won't give me my allowance this week." He said winking at her.

"Ben . . . stop teasing, you are going to be sleeping in the barn." She told him shaking her finger at him.

While he was gone, Karen and Melvin chatted about the market, the vendors and the things you could get there. She offered him cake but he said he was too full right now, so they decided to wait a little while. Ben came back into the room wiping his hands on a dish towel and said I'll finish them for you later."

"Thank you, Ben, for doing that you are a real sweetheart." She said.

"You're welcome, Hon. We're a team remember? Besides I enjoy sleeping in my own bed. I gotta earn those brownie points." He said grinning wide at her.

Melvin spoke up. "I wish my daughter had married someone like you Ben, so my farm would still be going. It took me years and years to build up the land, have a good productive herd and a nice milk check coming in each month. Now I don't have anything to do."

"Why didn't she want to stay in farming?" Karen asked.

"It was her husband, my son-in-law, he didn't care for it at all. He keeps talking to me about selling off plots of my land, well actually he talks about the whole farm now for vacation condos or a housing development of high-end homes. He's in real estate, but not very good at it I hear. I've got a small lake, it's actually just a large pond, but he said it could be the centerpiece of everything with a fountain in the middle shooting water in the air and houses perched around on the shore. He wants to call it Mountain Springs Development. Crazy idea, just to make money. These aren't mountains here, they're hills, and it wouldn't be a spring. It would be a cast iron pipe pumping water in the air. Stupid guy doesn't even know what a freshwater spring is. He even wants to put a golf course on my land, right through where my pastures and best planting fields were. There would be paved streets too for the houses. Pavement and concrete covering my land."

It was as if a dam had broken for Melvin's thoughts and he just kept talking. "He even wants to put an addition on my farmhouse and turn it into a clubhouse where they can serve cocktails for the golfers and members living in the development. It would be right where Grace had her kitchen garden and the perennial flowers she took such good care of. A bunch of them, the daylilies and the hollyhocks, are still blooming for me even though I don't know how to care for them. Can you imagine putting a building right on top of her garden? Grace will turn over in her grave if that happens. One of his worse suggestions is to tear down my barn and use the wood to panel that new addition. My good barn Ben. He wants to tear down my good barn!" Melvin was just shaking his head back and forth, his shoulders slumped over, and he was looking at the floor.

Feeling empathy for him, they sat silently just listening to his troubles as Melvin unloaded the burden and frustration, he had been carrying for so long. They could tell those drastic changes weighed so heavy on his heart.

"I know what you mean concerning the hope you had to pass the farm on to your daughter. We've been trying to build this farm up, so we can pass it on to our own children someday when we have them. We don't just do all this work for ourselves, it's to pass something on to them, to give them a head start. Not only the property but the lifestyle and it's values we love too." Ben said as Karen nodded her head right along with him.

"We've got problems here on our place now though and are starting to wonder if we can do that," Ben said.

Ben filled Melvin in on what had happened in the last couple years when the calves died and the toxic water on his farm. "Right now, Ben said, I've got a tanker of water parked for the stock and barn use and I'm buying water for the house too, but I can't keep doing it forever, it's too costly. We're in tandem trying to figure out what to do."

Melvin told them how sorry he was for their misfortune and hoped they could work out a way to keep farming there. They went out to sit on the porch to have a slice of the chocolate cake. Darkness was falling over the fields and they sat there looking at the deepening shadows of the buildings and trees as the sun was setting. Melvin finished his dessert and thanked them for such a pleasant evening. "Karen you've been so good to me sweetheart," he said.

"That's because you are such a honey," she said and hugged him. They both laughed as they realized she had called him "honey" despite his previous warning not to, but now it was okay. He told them again how grateful he was for the good meal, said goodnight, and got into his car. Karen and Ben watched as he slowly drove away.

"He's a lonely old man," Ben remarked as they went back into the house.

"I don't care for his son-in-law even though I've never met the man," Karen told him.

"Me either, and Melvin is so sad about having everything he's built up just go idle. His whole history there could be destroyed in the name of progress and making dollars." Ben answered, stretched his arms and yawned. "It's time to crash. Let's turn on the tv and snuggle for a while."

"Sounds good to me," Karen said as they headed for the living room.

Chapter Eleven

AFTER MELVIN had left Karen and Ben sat talking on the sofa about what their life might be like when they were his age.

"By then we should have three or four children and grandchildren too, shouldn't we?" Karen asked.

"Yes, and I'll be milking at least triple what I'm doing now," Ben said. "I've been thinking I'm going to start a herd of beef cattle in the near future. I've got enough pasture. They don't take as much attention as the dairy cows and beef gets a good price right now. We just have to get this water problem figured out." Ben still hadn't accepted the fact that he might have to abandon his father's farm.

"I'm considering expanding my bake goods business, Ben. I want to package my cookies in cute little boxes with black and white Holstein patterns and put them in places such as the health food store or the diner. I should get some branding down too, have a logo designed and come up with a name, maybe the Farmer's Oven or Country Crumbs or something catchy." Karen said.

"We're just starting on our adventure Karen. We're going to do really good and we have so much ahead of us yet." He hugged Karen close and kissed her forehead. "I feel sorry for Melvin though. At this point in his life he doesn't have much to look forward to does he except getting older? And that son-in-law of his wants to take everything familiar to him away. I'll bet gets him feeling depressed and sad."

Karen was listening to what Ben was saying and how Melvin had talked before he left. She remembered hearing about the vendor whose father had taken his life. Suddenly she sat upright.

"Oh, my God. Ben, I think Melvin is going to hurt himself! I've got a bad feeling. I need to call him and ask if he got home okay."

"Karen, it's getting late. He'd be in bed by now."

"Ben, I can't explain it, I've got to call him." She got her phone and punched in his number. The phone rang and rang. There was no answer even from a machine. "Ben, he should be home by now to answer his phone." She said worriedly.

"Maybe he doesn't answer late calls, my parents didn't. He could already be in bed and doesn't want to get up." Ben told her. "Why are you so worried?"

"I don't know Ben. It was the things he said like not being needed anymore and something in his voice when he said goodbye tonight. Almost as if he didn't plan on seeing me again, like it was final. Maybe I'm overreacting and being silly, but we should go over there and check on him." She got up and headed for the kitchen. I'll take some more leftovers and tell him we forgot to give them to him as an excuse. Come on Ben, this is important. I'll explain it more in the car."

"All right, if we can come back home and go to bed afterwards. I gotta get some rest Hon and I'm looking forward to cuddling with you." Ben grabbed his keys and they headed for their truck.

Melvin drove home very slowly after dinner. His mind was full of thoughts of the times when he and Grace were young the same as those two were, and had full busy lives building their farm up and raising their daughter. He thought of how empty his days were now and how he never had much to do to fill them. There were no demands on his time now to do any physical work which was good at his age, but at the same time, he didn't believe he was needed by anyone, man or animal. The dairy had relied on him to be there for long hours every day. If he didn't milk those cows on time twice a day, they would suffer and be ruined as milkers. It had been necessary for him to be there at a certain time, day after day no matter even if he didn't feel like doing it or he was ill, it had to be done, no excuses. Now it didn't even matter how late he slept or what he did to keep himself busy each day. No one needed him or required anything from him.

He loved his daughter, but she had a busy life of her own and had grown into a strong independent woman except when it came to her husband. She caved in to his demands too much Melvin thought.

"That damn man," Melvin said talking to the empty seat in the car. "Grace, I can't stand our son-in-law planning to tear up our farm, but I won't be able to stop it if he has his way. I know he's waiting for me to kick off or talk me into his plans before I do. He probably wants to move me into a nursing home or trailer park."

He thought about the Power of Attorney he had given his daughter a few years ago in case his mind got a little feeble, so she could make financial decisions and health choices for him.

'You know Grace our son-in-law could talk her into using those papers to take away my farm now." He said out loud. "He's shrewd and greedy enough to do it."

The more Melvin considered his current situation the more despondent he felt. He pulled into his driveway and noticed he had forgotten to turn on the porch light. He sat in the car looking at the dark silhouette of the farmhouse he had spent so many years in. There was no sign of life anywhere. No lights streaming out of the windows because Grace was no longer inside waiting for him. No dog barking to welcome him and let Grace know he had arrived home. His old farm dog was gone too. No smells of a home cooked meal such as when he had pulled up to Karen's porch earlier or the sounds of cows mooing in the barn waiting to be milked.

He felt the tremendous weight of loneliness pushing him on down and he slumped in the car seat. He and Grace had worked so hard for most of their married life to grow and add to the farm and raise their daughter. Now, this last part of his life was loss. The loss of his wife, the loss of his dairy business, the loss of his daughter to marriage and now the loss of his health too and worse of all the loss of having a purpose in life. He stepped out of the car and closed the door behind him. He noticed the old vehicle was starting to get rust on it now and thought of how happy he and Grace had been when they bought it new so many years before. She had picked the color out.

"I'd want it to be Robin's Egg Blue Melvin." She had said. "Wouldn't it be fun to ride in a car the color of those pretty eggshells? But don't ever crack it up." She said joking.

"Me crack it up?" Warren had answered. "You're the one who ran over the mailbox with our other car remember!"

Warren smiled now remembering those times. He rubbed a small dent in the fender where Grace had dinged it from a close encounter with a deer. Thank God she wasn't hurt he said to himself. I miss her so much. I miss it all so much. Warren walked up onto the porch, opened his door and switched on the light. Everything regarding the house was so familiar to him now he could have left the light off. The kitchen was on the right, the living room on the left, the bathroom down the hall. He noticed a mouse scurry along the baseboard and thought *I should set a trap* but didn't move to get one. Every piece of furniture, every number of steps it took to walk here or there in the house or barn was programmed into his body.

He took off his jacket, hung it on a hook and walked down the hallway. On the way, he passed the gun cabinet with his old familiar rifle standing silently behind the gleaming glass. He reached above the cabinet for the key hidden there and unlocked the door. It swung open by itself. He didn't even think about it; he reached in and touched the gun as if he was reaching to shake the hand of an old friend. He lifted it from the cabinet and stroked the polished dark mahogany wood of its handle.

"You've helped me get several rabbits and deer for the pot haven't you old fellow?" He asked the gun as if it could answer. Then he answered for it. "Yup, we've taken lots of trips to the old woods, together didn't we?" He closed the cabinet door, locked it and put the key back in its hiding place, but not before he grabbed a couple of shells off the top shelf.

He paused to look at the pictures hanging in the hallway of he and Grace, there were lots of pictures too of their daughter as she was growing up. Pictures of Grace holding their daughter as a baby. Photos of their daughter as a little girl on her new bike, and pictures of her with calves and the 4H blue ribbons at the fair. He looked at her graduation pictures and the more recent ones from a few years ago of her marriage with Grace standing beside her. He kissed his fingertips and then touched the photo of both with them. He stepped back out onto the porch, turned off the house light and sat in his favorite chair. He slid the shells into the gun, closed it and lay it across his knees. He looked out into the dark at what he could see of his barns and fields and listened intently for any familiar sounds of the cows, but still, there was none. He thought of his parents long gone, and the brother and sister he had outlived too and Grace waiting for him.

When Ben and Karen drove up and parked their truck, he was just sitting in his chair on the porch. There was no movement. Karen gasped and said "Oh, my God no." Then she saw Melvin's arm come up as he shielded his eyes from their headlights. Who the heck would be coming to my house this time of night he wondered. He couldn't make out who it was at first. Relieved when he moved, they got out of their truck and walked up the steps. Karen was carrying the leftovers. They both noticed the gun in his lap right away.

"Melvin, what on earth are you doing out here in the dark with a rifle?" Ben asked.

Taking time to answer he said, "I thought I heard an animal prowling around."

Ben and Karen turned and looked around the yard. "Well, there's nothing here now Melvin, we would have seen it in our headlights if there was. Is that thing loaded?" Ben asked.

Again, Melvin was slow to answer. "Yes, it's got a couple shells in it."

"Can I see your old gun Melvin; it looks like a good one," Ben said as he reached over and took it. Melvin's eyes were tearful as he let Ben take the gun away.

"You know mine's not working good lately, the sights are way off, and I've got an intruder coming into the hayloft of the barn at night trying to kill the pigeons. Could be a bobcat, but whatever it is it's spooking the cows too. Do you mind if I borrow this for a couple days Melvin?" Ben asked him.

Slowly, measuring every word Melvin answered him. "Well, I guess I wouldn't need it for a few more days anyways."

Karen sat down in a chair beside the old man and took his hand. "Melvin we sure did enjoy your visit tonight and want you to come back again. Ben needs a person with your experience to talk to. You have learned so much farming all those years and can give him good advice. My dad has passed on too, the same as his and I love talking to you at the market on Saturdays and we both want to get to know you better. We need someone with your knowledge in our life, don't we Ben?"

"Yes, we certainly do. I have so many questions for you Melvin, I need your advice on how I could expand the farm and so much more." Ben told him.

"You do?" Melvin asked looking at him.

"Yes, for sure Melvin. What you know we can't find in books." Karen reached over and hugged him.

"I enjoy talking to you too," Melvin said quietly. They sat there in silence for a few minutes not saying what was really on their minds.

Karen spoke. "Melvin I've heard stories concerning older farmers who get very lonely and they don't want to live anymore." She paused considering how to tactfully but firmly say what she wanted to him. "Melvin, promise me if you ever get discouraged, you'll talk to me or someone else, please. Can you promise me that? I want to be sure you have someone to talk to if you get feeling sad regarding anything. We're your friends now and we will be here if you need us. Please promise me you'll call us, even if it does sound silly to you Melvin."

Melvin's face transformed into a warmer more engaged look as he turned to Karen to answer her. "You have been a good friend Karen." He said, "And I always look forward to seeing you, and Ben, I would like to get to know you both better too and tell you what I can. Yes, I promise I'll call you if I need anything."

"Great," Karen replied. "Now here's a few more leftovers, we still had way too many. Show me where I can put these away for you please."

Melvin rose from his chair and led Karen inside to the kitchen. When he passed Grace's picture hanging on the wall, he thought he saw her smiling at him.

Chapter Twelve

THE NEXT day Ben talked with Karen about what he and Warren were going to do to bring Coleman to justice and get help for them too. She helped him go over the evidence of dumping they already had accumulated. They could use the pictures Warren had taken at the cabin of the charts and the deliveries. They had the water tests from the EnBioApp lab in Mansfield and could probably get the Water truck driver, Keith Tynor's testimony. The way to assure Blair Coleman got prosecuted they thought, would be to record incriminating statements from him, it's what Ben wanted and had decided to get.

Warren called and told Ben he had a meeting with Coleman at the Elmira plant. Blair Coleman was eager to have him visit he said and let him know what MetInverse Enterprises could do for his new business and make it profitable. They had two days to figure out how to record the conversation and nail Coleman with enough evidence to bring legal action against him and stop him from what he was doing. Warren told Ben it was simple, all he had to do was, set his cell phone to record, leave it in his shirt pocket the same as he usually did, and they were good to go.

Warren had the appearance of a new business owner when he showed up at Coleman's plant in Elmira and handed him a professional looking business card Karen had printed the night before. They shook hands and Warren told Blair, he had started a company refurbishing office copiers and large printers after which he resold them at a good price. He got so much into his role he even tried to sell Coleman one of his fantasy refurbished office copiers. Warren asked to see the plant operations and Coleman agreed. He walked him through a hallway then opened a door marked *Authorized Personnel Only.* It led to the working part of the plant.

"You know usually no one comes back here. Too many ways to get hurt, however, I'll make an exception for you. You wouldn't sue me if something happened would you partner?" Coleman asked jokingly. Warren had a hard time keeping a straight face at that remark, but answered: "No way, not me, I hate those damn lawyers."

Coleman showed him machine casings they were working on, how they looked when they came in and the steps they traveled through soaking in the various large chemical tanks. Some finishes, he said, required reverse electroplating to get the finish back off where the stripping chemicals were charged with an electric current. Warren could see fumes rising off the nasty chemical baths. The workmen had masks on covering their nose and mouths, plus heavy rubber gloves and goggles to protect their eyes. Then Coleman spotted one who didn't have his mask on and shouted "Get your damn mask back on. I don't want OSHA coming in here and giving me another fine." Warren thought Coleman seemed more concerned about getting a fine than his employee's health. Warren asked if they used the same liquids more than one time and Coleman told Warren "Yes, until they get so thick with residue, we can't filter it out to make it usable anymore."

"What do you do with it when that happens?" He asked.

"Oh, it's disposed of at a landfill made for chemical waste," Coleman said as he looked away.

The plant was busy with lots of different casings and machine parts loaded onto big wire mesh trays suspended overhead on chains. Workers moved them along on an overhead track and then lowered the trays of parts into big vats of paint stripping chemicals to sit for a while. Other workers were raising trays back out, so they hung suspended over the vats dripping stripping chemicals. The acrid smell of the liquids was heavy in the air. Warren noticed most of the workers looked as if they came from South America and thought Coleman had made an ethnic choice with the majority of his job force too. He wondered why.

The back door by the docks was open and Warren could see a red truck parked at it with the Hazmat signs on it. Same set up as Mansfield he thought.

Coleman finished his tour and said, "Let's go back into my office to talk business."

When they reached the reception area Warren asked him, "Could you give me a minute while I make a quick call? My business partner was supposed to meet me here; however, he's running a little late. I want him to be in on our discussion."

"No problem," Coleman said, "when he gets here have my secretary let me know and we'll finish up with what we need to talk about." He told his secretary to bring coffee for all of them when the partner arrived. Coleman returned to the comforts of his plush air-conditioned office and Warren made a quick call to Ben to come on into the building to have a sit down with Coleman. He quickly checked his phone to make sure it was set to record.

Ben went right in; he'd been waiting for that call. That day he'd gotten dressed up in a shirt and tie resembling a professional businessman too. The secretary told Coleman the partner had arrived then showed them into Coleman's office. Before she left Coleman reminded her to bring his guests coffee again.

Warren introduced Ben as his partner, Coleman shook his hand then paused and asked, "Wait a minute, don't I know you?"

Ben spoke "Yes, you do Mr. Coleman, I'm your neighbor, you outbid me on the property next to my farm. You have a hunting cabin above my place Hillside Farm."

Coleman looked puzzled then thinking for a moment he said "Oh, so you're in this new business venture with Warren?" he asked.

"No, not exactly," Ben answered smiling, then his expression changed and became quite serious. "There actually is no new business. We're here to find out why you're dumping toxic chemicals down a well you had drilled." Everything was still in the office. You could hear the clock on the wall ticking. Coleman's smile suddenly disappeared, and he backed away from them.

He put both hands up into the air and was shaking his head. "Whoa, I don't know where this is coming from. I dispose of the liquids we use in this operation properly. We get inspected several times during the year and pass." He sat down at his desk. On the wall behind him were awards from the Rotary Club and the Better Business Association. There were pictures of a Little League Team he sponsored and Youth Football.

"You're a liar," Ben said. "We know exactly how you are dumping them illegally and where. What I want to know is why, why are you doing a stupid thing?"

Coleman was still trying to cover up. "I told you I don't know what information you have; you're mistaken. We conform to all industry standards."

"You're still lying." Ben was close to him shouting now. "We talked to Keith Tynor, the man you hired to haul the stripping chemicals away, we have printouts recording the gallons he's dumped in Pennsylvania. We know about the trucks parked out back of your plants that go nowhere. We know everything Blair except the why, why are you doing this?" Ben asked again. The door opened, and the secretary stood there with coffee cups on a tray and a bewildered look on her face.

Coleman barked at her "Not now!" so she quickly put the tray down, turned around went back out the door.

Coleman had his hands on the top of his desk and was looking down at papers there. "My business employs several people around here. I bring money to these small towns; my employees live in the area."

Warren didn't care for that remark and said "They may live in the area now because you brought them here, but they're not from the area. I'll bet you hired them for cheap, under the table labor instead of hiring local people and paying a decent wage. You're probably not paying them health benefits or anything else."

Coleman looked frustrated "You think I'm the only one dumping industrial chemicals? There is plenty of us who have used industrial fluids to get rid of, and the state and feds have made it too expensive and too complicated to take it to the landfill. There's dry cleaners, and auto finishers, factories, screen printers, research labs even your damn local car repair shop has stuff to dump like antifreeze, steering, and brake fluid. Wake up fellows it's a chemical world you have to learn to live in it!"

"That's just it," Ben said, "we won't live in a world with chemical crap polluting everything."

Coleman was still fuming, "Those fracking guys dump bad stuff down wells all the time and the government gives them their blessing. They don't even have to tell anyone what they are using or dumping down the wells they drill because of the Halliburton Loophole. "

"What the hell is the Halliburton Loophole?" Warren asked.

Ben told him "It's part of the Energy Bill passed in 2005. The EPA has no authority over the Fracking Companies. They can dump used chemicals down deep wells and don't have to say what chemical combinations they have used to frack, and they can't be sued by anyone. Former Vice President Cheney headed an Energy Task Force and had it added to the bill before it passed. He used to be Chief Executive of Halliburton, a company involved in oil and gas."

Coleman continued complaining, "I should be allowed the same privileges as those fracking guys. Do you have any idea of the costs to get rid of these stripping chemicals from my plant? First, there's treatment, storage and disposal permits that can run up to $30,000 plus Environmental License Fees. Then there's Program Fees and fees to have people Hazmat trained including the truck driver's and everyone that works on the line, then Special Assessment and Inspection Fees. Plus, there's fines, if they notice anything such as a worker with a glove off or an exhaust fan not working, or a spill not cleaned up perfectly. And there's other Special Landfill Fees and more fees added if it's put into a separate Chemical Surface Impoundment. It goes on and on, and those fees are every damn year, not just a onetime thing! I'm trying to make a profit here. So, why shouldn't I, as a small businessman, be allowed the same privileges as the fracking guys? I'm not a big corporation with lots of financial resources and all kinds of tax breaks they have, I'm a small businessman." Coleman was angry and shaking his head, he reached for the fat cigar he had smoldering in an ashtray.

"Why?" Ben answered so furious he was having problems not punching Coleman in the face. "Because you poisoned my water, made my wife sick and killed my calves you S.O.B. We can't even drink what comes out of our kitchen faucet on our family farm. A farm my father worked hard on all his life, so he could hand it down to me. You've poisoned it all and you didn't have to. You did it because you loved the dollar over your fellow man. I'm taking the information we have on you and your company to the EPA and the newspapers and I'm getting a lawyer to sue you for damages. You act as if you can do what you want, but you're not exempt and you're going to pay for this, you're not going to get away with it." Ben slammed his fist on Coleman's desk.

Coleman said "It's not my fault your water is polluted. Herrick told me that well was deep enough."

Warren straightened up at that remark and asked "Professor Herrick? What's the hell has he got to do with all this?"

"He owns a share of this business," Coleman fired back, then realizing he shouldn't have shared that information his face turned red.

Ben spoke again "Well, I'll be damned. So, you two put your heads together and planned how to dump the toxic chemicals from your refurbishing plants. You both had a financial reason for this coverup. This is priceless."

Coleman stood up and told them to get out. He said neither of them knew what they were talking about and this conversation was over.

Ben said angrily, "We're done talking, but you haven't seen the last of me." He and Warren left the office and slammed the door behind them. Outside his office, the secretary was huddled with another employee and they both looked worried as the angry men walked through the reception area and out the front door. Back in the pickup Warren checked his phone and started playing the recorded conversation back. They were elated after hearing Coleman repeat "I'm not the only one dumping industrial chemicals." And later in the recording, they heard him say "Herrick said my well was deep enough." They gave each other a high five and whooped in joy at the evidence the cell phone had captured. "Gotchya Scumbag!" Ben said.

"What now?" Warren asked. "Time for a beer?"

"Well, I'm going to do exactly what I told Coleman. I'll contact the EPA and they can shut him down for a while at least and fine him. I hear it's a stiff fine, especially since he's crossed state lines. There was another plant owner who got fined $15 million in federal court for improperly storing and disposing of hazardous waste. He was given five years in prison too. I'm sure they will bring criminal charges against Coleman and probably Herrick too. I'm passing our information on to the newspaper also, and they are going to love this story. I can see the headlines now *Upstanding Citizen Spreads Poison.* I've never sued anyone; however, I'm going to contact my lawyer and get damages from Coleman and Herrick for what they've done to Karen and me, so we can start over."

"Ben, I don't think you can get the pollution back out of the ground on your farm. Your water is never going to be good again, you know. He dumped those toxic paint stripping solutions and shit like that." Warren said sadly.

Ben's shoulders slumped, "I know that Warren the lab tech said it was soluble, heavy metals which would sink and stay in the soil and water source. My father's farm is ruined. I wouldn't dare stay there in the dairy business and raise my own kids there too with that toxic soup in the groundwater. I probably can't even sell the place now." Ben let out a long sigh and looked out the truck window off into the distance towards the hills.

Warren asked, "Ben, where will you and Karen go, you're not giving up farming are you?"

"We'll look for a place far enough from Coleman's well to be safe, yet not too far from your farm. After all, we still share Lightning you know, and he can't travel far. He's got to save his energy to romance the ladies." Ben laughed.

"Yeah, he sure does like to woo the moo and that's no bull," Warren said grinning. Ben groaned and shook his head.

"Besides, Ben went on, I should be able to get enough for a good settlement from MetInverse Enterprises to buy a bigger farm and start the milking operation I always wanted. I might even be able to hire the help I'll need. We'll be okay, Karen and I."

"I know you will Ben. You've got Karen and the desire to work hard and do things the right way. You'll be okay, I'm sure of it."

Ben nodded his head confidently, "Yes, we're just going to ride the float for a while until everything smooths out."

Later that evening Ben and Karen were talking over what their next step would be. It was costing too much to buy tankers of water for the herd and more water for the house and they both knew they couldn't keep doing it. They were considering selling off the herd and renting an apartment to get away from the toxic water. It would give them the money they needed to file their lawsuit. They could store their machinery at Warren's farm until they got funds to buy another farm someplace and more cows from the settlement they hoped to get. It all sounded as if it could take a long time. Ben would have to get another job for a while if they did move though. Right now, everything looked gloomy and uncertain for them it was so depressing to talk about giving up completely on the farm and their dreams.

The phone rang, and Ben answered it to the sound of Melvin's voice. He said "Ben, I've been thinking a lot about how my son-in-law wants to replace my farm with a development and your water predicament over there. You said there's no way to make your water healthy again?" Melvin asked.

"That's right Melvin. We found out filters won't even take all the chemicals out." Ben answered.

"Well, Ben I believe I should sell my farm to you and Karen if you want it, and I'll take the money and give it to my daughter for her inheritance. It's a way this good land over here won't be all tore up and destroyed and you'll have a great place to farm and expand your operation. I've got a lot more acres over here. How do you like that idea?"

Ben had turned on the speakerphone when Melvin called, and Karen had been listening too. She spoke up. "Melvin, we won't have any money to do anything until we get a settlement from the lawsuit we're going to file. It could take some time."

"That's alright," Melvin said. "I'd consider you caretakers of my property while you lived here, and you could stay for free. Then when you get your settlement you can buy my farm for a reasonable price. I'd really want you to do that Ben. I might even be able to drive the tractor for you once in a while or help with milking in the barn. It'd ease my mind to know the farm would be going again and keep being a farm in the future and not a damn housing development. Would you consider the idea Ben?"

Karen and Ben smiled at each other not believing how much their luck had just changed. She nodded her head yes at Ben and he said “Melvin it sounds like such a wonderful, generous offer. I don’t think we could turn it down. It would ease my mind a lot to get Karen and our animals away from here. I love this place but it’s ruined. We’d be happy to take you up on your offer.”

“Good,” Melvin said. “And I’ll have the benefit of Karen’s good cooking too. Let’s get together soon and work it all out. Give me a call after you consider it a little more. Goodnight to both of you and Karen I’ll talk to you Saturday at the market when I get my loaf of your homemade bread and my cookies.”

Ben hung up the phone and turned to Karen. She had tears running down her face and he wrapped her in his arms and held her close. Everything was going to smooth out, it would be bumpy for some time, but they were going to be okay.

About the Author

DORIS WILBUR is an author living in rural New York State who writes about historical events as well as stories inspired by modern day headlines. The settings and events in her stories are infused with nature, including the plants, animals and landscapes of the areas, and give you a vivid sense of place. Her characters face many challenges both natural and man-made. She creates a captivating story as they cope with feelings, choices and events to overcome those challenges.

Doris spent much of her career as a graphic artist and award-winning watercolor artist. She was a public-school art teacher also, but behind the scenes she always wrote. She has worked for newspapers, advertising agencies, school systems, and had a graphic design business.

She and her husband Jerry raised five children and have lived in New York State, Pennsylvania, Maryland, and Florida. She grew up on a small dairy farm but has also lived and worked in the large cities of Washington, DC; Orlando, Florida; and Syracuse, New York.

She graduated summa cum laude from Mansfield University of Pennsylvania where she studied Creative Writing, Botany and Art Education. Now, she and her husband live at a private lake surrounded by the woods and nature that she loves where she continues to teach and write.

Doris has another book, *A Lenape Legacy*, published by Sunbury Press. It's the story of a young colonial girl who was captured by the Indians and was assimilated into their culture.

CPSIA information can be obtained
at www.ICGtesting.com
Printed in the USA
LVHW021049111119
636959LV00007B/2743